"You're my boss, not my boyfriend."

"The two are not mutually exclusive, Ashley," replied Gray, who was still holding on to her hand and watching her with that maddening little grin.

"Yes, they are," Ashley said, while trying desperately to pull away from him. "Can we go?"

To her enormous relief, he released her and allowed her to drag her coat from the cupboard. Then he pulled her arm through his and marched her out of the door with almost military briskness.

"So you don't have a boyfriend?" mused Gray.

"No," she said shortly.

He was still bent toward her, his eyes glittering close to her own. "How did that happen? Pigheadedness, bad manners or bad management?"

"Luck."

Kay Gregory grew up in England, but moved to Canada as a teenager. She now lives in Vancouver with her husband, two sons, one dog and two ferrets. She has had innumerable jobs that have often provided background for her books. Now that she is writing Harlequin romance novels, Kay thinks she has at last found a job that she won't find necessary to change.

Books by Kay Gregory

HARLEQUIN ROMANCE
3016—A PERFECT BEAST
3058—IMPULSIVE BUTTERFLY
3082—AMBER AND AMETHYST
3152—YESTERDAY'S WEDDING
3206—BREAKING THE ICE
3243—AFTER THE ROSES

HARLEQUIN PRESENTS
1352—THE MUSIC OF LOVE

RAINBOW OF LOVE
Kay Gregory

Harlequin Books

TORONTO • NEW YORK • LONDON
AMSTERDAM • PARIS • SYDNEY • HAMBURG
STOCKHOLM • ATHENS • TOKYO • MILAN
MADRID • WARSAW • BUDAPEST • AUCKLAND

With my love
To BOB, who is the ultimate hero, not only for his
unfailing support when my confidence has been at
a low ebb, but also because he can cook!

ISBN 0-373-17179-X

RAINBOW OF LOVE

Copyright © 1992 by Kay Gregory.

This edition published by arrangement with Harlequin Enterprises B. V.

® and TM are trademarks of the publisher. Trademarks indicated with
® are registered in the United States Patent and Trademark Office, the
Canadian Trade Marks Office and in other countries.

Printed in U.S.A.

CHAPTER ONE

"Do you always serve the customer who makes the most noise first?" inquired Gray bitingly, as he contemplated the not unpleasant vision of shapely legs under a neat navy blue bottom perched halfway up a ladder against the wall. "Or is it a matter of first come last served in this establishment?"

Ashley started, and almost fell off her perch as she grabbed for a pair of hiking boots in his size before sliding awkwardly to the floor. She staggered, still clutching the boots, as he extended a black-clad arm to pull her upright.

"What?" she gasped, flustered and disconcerted, by his closeness as much as by his words. "I'm sorry, I don't understand..."

Gray rolled his eyes up and muttered impatiently, "Oh, Lord! Dumb as well as disorganized!"

Among her friends and relatives Ashley was known to be remarkably even-tempered. It was also generally accepted that she maintained her good humor by refusing to let life's injuries and irritations fester. In other words, if someone stepped on her toes or made her angry, they were very soon made aware of it.

"I am not dumb, Mr. McGraw," she said tightly, "nor am I particularly disorganized. You, on the other hand, are extremely rude."

"Am I, now?" he murmured, eyeing her slim figure appraisingly as she backed away from him. When she reached a row of chairs along the wall, he added with a note of what she could have sworn was disillusion, "So

5

you did recognize me, then, did you? I might have known.''

"Yes, of course I recognized you," replied Ashley. "You happen to own the most famous face in Thunder Bay." When he continued to regard her with that intent, deliberately insulting gaze, she continued, "I just wasn't impressed, I'm afraid."

It was true. She had known who he was the moment he came into the store. He wasn't the sort of person one overlooked, but she had been determined not to show any special interest. She had never been impressed by sports heroes of any kind, because most of the ones she'd encountered had been thoroughly impressed with themselves. As far as she could see, Gray McGraw was no exception. Apart from which, she had always thought hockey players looked more ridiculous than sexy in their bulky padded uniforms and space-age helmets—an attitude which she knew put her out of step with the majority of her compatriots in this land where hockey was a national obsession.

"Hmm," he grunted, with a speculative hardness in his eye that made her wary. "What was that you said about rudeness? And incidentally, in my book it's bad manners *and* bad business to leave one customer high and dry while you dash off to serve another."

Twin spots of color appeared on Ashley's high cheekbones. "For your information, Mr. McGraw, Mrs. Cartwright was here before you were."

"You could have fooled me. At two hundred pounds and wearing a tight pink pantsuit, the lady was hardly invisible. You'd think I'd have noticed her, wouldn't you?"

Ashley tried not to grind her teeth. "I mean she'd been in three times already today, and her son's skates still hadn't been sent over from the warehouse. You can't really blame her for being a little impatient."

"No, but I can blame you for walking off to take care of her when you were supposed to be looking after me."

She stared at him, noting the powerful frame in the sheepskin-lined black leather jacket, the long legs in tight black jeans, and the whole alluring specimen of virility which was topped off by the sort of face that attracted women like moths toward a flame—or like flies to fly-paper, she amended acidly. Still...freed from the trappings of his trade, there was no getting away from it. Gray McGraw, lord of the rinks, and one of Canada's most spectacular and brilliant hockey forwards, was a very nice hunk of man. Thick dark hair worn rather long, a nose that had obviously been broken at one time—which only added to his attraction—full sensual lips, a firm jaw, and eyes so dark and deep one could drown in their brooding black depths. Yes, and brooding they definitely were as they settled on her own elfin features. Not that she cared for intense, dark good looks, she reminded herself hastily. She much preferred fair hair, blue eyes and nice friendly smiles.

To her confusion, and as if he had read her thoughts, at that moment Gray began to smile. But it wasn't a friendly smile. And it certainly wasn't nice. On the contrary, it was cool, supercilious and, she was sure, quite clearly intended to provoke. "Well?" he drawled, gesturing at the boots she still held clutched in her hand. "If it isn't too much trouble, do you think you might find the time to finish the job? Assuming you've nothing more pressing in mind, naturally. Or is that too much to ask?"

The spots of color spread to the rest of her face. At the moment, what she longed to do more than anything was to bring both hiking boots down smartly on Gray McGraw's high-and-mighty head. But Mr. Boyko wouldn't like that. Mr. Boyko owned this sporting goods shop and twenty others across eastern Canada, as well as the main distributorship on the edge of town, and he took a dim view of employees who annoyed customers—especially customers as rich and influential as Gray McGraw.

Ashley sighed inwardly. Hitting this obnoxious man on the head would undoubtedly be classified as unacceptable. And she had been working here on Friday nights and Saturdays for the last five years specifically because she needed the money.

She still did. Besides, she had to admit that, although it would be enormously satisfying, it really wasn't professional to assault customers with the merchandise they were in the process of buying.

Swallowing her pride, she waved at one of the chairs. "Won't you have a seat?" she asked woodenly. "I'll be right with you."

Gray raised his eyebrows and managed to look both disbelieving and seductive at the same time. But he did as she suggested, and lowered his long body into a green plastic chair, which immediately assumed the proportions of dolls' furniture. Ashley wondered if he always made everything around him seem smaller. She suspected he did, and it didn't endear him to her one bit.

Not for the first time, she mentally cursed Mr. Boyko for neglecting to provide stools for his shoe departments. The last thing she wanted to do at this moment was grovel at the Great McGraw's feet. But there was no help for it. Catching her bottom lip firmly between her teeth, she knelt down to remove his black running shoes.

There was a very large hole in his socks.

Ashley's eyes lit with a gleam of malicious satisfaction. So the man was human after all.

She had meant to keep her gaze unfalteringly fixed on his feet, but, without intending to, she found herself glancing upward.

He was watching her with a slight crease between his heavy eyebrows, and the cool smile still played around his mouth. She had a feeling he knew exactly how much she disliked her present subservient position, and was thoroughly enjoying her discomfiture. And he didn't give a damn about his socks. Her eyes dropped back to his feet as she eased the soft leather boots up over his solid male ankles.

"Very nice," he observed, when she had finished. "Neat. I like them."

The instant he opened his mouth she became aware that the top button on her blouse was missing—and she knew that his approving comment had nothing whatever to do with boots. Blushing scarlet, Ashley jumped to her feet and, mumbling something about being back in just a minute, scuttled into the storeroom to find one of the safety pins she always carried prudently in her bag. In no time at all, and respectably fastened to the neck again, she was back in the main store facing Gray—who was still sitting in the green chair with his legs stretched out, and looking more superior than ever.

"You deserted me again," he remarked without inflection. "Tell me, what does it take to make you stick to the job?"

"In your case, glue," snapped Ashley, goaded beyond endurance or any thought whatever for Mr. Boyko's rules regarding customer relations. "If you don't mind, Mr. McGraw, it's closing time, so if those boots aren't just what you want——"

"But I do mind. And they are."

Ashley clenched her teeth. "In that case I'll ring them up for you if you'll take them off." She extended a commanding hand.

But Gray wasn't easily commanded. "Aren't you going to take them off for me?" he asked laconically. There was a glint of sheer incitement in his eye.

"No," said Ashley, taking a deep breath, "I'm not."

"I wonder why that is," he murmured, the glint becoming more pronounced than ever. "I rather enjoy watching you on your knees. You have quite an appealing neck beneath that glossy black helmet of hair. Did you know that?"

Ashley glared. "My neck's none of your business," she said shortly, recollecting that Gray McGraw had a reputation for having an unusual way with words, and wishing she could be equally effective.

"Isn't it?" he replied mildly. "What a pity. It's really quite a nice neck——"

"Mr. McGraw," hissed Ashley, "will you please hand me those boots? And then will you please get out of my shop?"

"Aha, so the lady has a temper." He grinned aggravatingly. "As a matter of fact, I thought this was Charlie Boyko's business." When her slanting dark eyes flashed bright daggers at him he grinned again.

"It is Mr. Boyko's," she replied frostily. "The boots, please, Mr. McGraw."

Gray, apparently deciding he'd gone far enough, removed the boots and handed them to her with surprising and suspicious meekness. "I'm glad you said 'please,'" he told her, spoiling any sense of triumph she might have felt.

Ashley didn't answer. Instead she walked briskly to the cash register and began to ring in his purchase. He followed her more slowly and leaned casually up against the counter.

Ashley, with one last vicious jab at the keypad, grabbed the money he offered and then slammed the drawer shut with a bang. "Your boots," she said loftily, handing him his neatly wrapped package. With more willpower than she had known she possessed, she managed not to add, And I hope they give you blisters.

"Thank you," said Gray quite pleasantly. "It's been a pleasure, Miss...?"

She ignored him.

"Don't you have a name?" he inquired conversationally. "Or is it just that you don't want me to know it?"

Oh, what the hell. If he wanted to complain to Mr. Boyko, he would do so, name or no name. "It's Ashley," she told him curtly. "Ashley Kalani."

"I might have known."

She paused in the act of pulling the cover over the cash register.

"Known what?"

"That it would be something improbable and unpronounceable."

"It's not improbable. Joe Ashley was my father's best man. And don't pretend you can't pronounce Kalani—even you should be able to manage that."

"Thanks for the vote of confidence," he said, smiling innocently. "You're right, of course. I just wanted to see your eyes flash. Thank you, Ashley. This afternoon has proved much more entertaining than I expected."

"Great. My afternoon's been bloody awful!" Ashley shouted after him.

But it was too late. He had already closed the door.

"Rough day?" inquired Toivo Kalani, peering at his daughter's drawn and peaky face over the top of his newspaper.

"You could put it that way." Ashley plumped herself down in an overstuffed chair in the corner of her parents' big, comfortable kitchen, and for once she was thankful that she still lived at home and didn't have to go to a solitary apartment and make decisions about what to have for supper.

"What happened?" asked Rosa Kalani, turning quickly around from the stove.

"Oh, nothing much. It was busy most of the day, and that order of skates didn't come in until late, which put half a dozen customers in a bad mood—including Mrs. Cartwright..."

"Uh-huh. And what else?" Rosa knew her daughter well.

Ashley shrugged. "The Great White Big Deal came in."

Her father put down the paper and stifled a chuckle. "The Great White *what*?"

"Gray McGraw. In person."

"Ah. Never met him. His visit wasn't a success, then?"

"It was a disaster."

"Hmm. Want to tell us about it?"

Ashley did, and, when she had finished, her father's lined but still distinguished face registered a puzzled disbelief. "I'm surprised," he murmured mildly. "You're usually so good at smoothing ruffled feathers." His gaze strayed back to the paper, and Ashley stood up and went to help her mother peel potatoes.

"You look like a wet day in November," remarked Rosa, her dark eyes maternal and concerned.

"Well, it is November," her daughter pointed out reasonably. "And it is raining."

"Doesn't mean you have to look like it." Rosa continued to regard her daughter with concern, and eventually she asked thoughtfully, "That McGraw—was he *really* angry?"

"Well, he was at first, I think, and I can't altogether blame him—although I'd like to. I shouldn't have left him standing there, but I was tired and not thinking clearly, and Mrs. Cartwright——"

"Hah!" Toivo interrupted, thumping the paper down onto the table. "Did you see this? Might explain it."

"See what?" queried Ashley.

"The latest bulletin on McGraw. Seems he'll never play major league hockey again. The doctors have finally pronounced it hopeless. He's retiring."

"Oh-h!" exclaimed Ashley, dropping the potato peeler and sitting down suddenly. "I wonder—no, that couldn't be why he was in such a filthy mood. He must have known for ages it was likely."

"Mmm," agreed Toivo, "you're right. McGraw's the kind of man who'd take it on the chin. Too bad, though. He's only twenty-nine, and the game's been his whole life up to now. One of the toughest and most aggressive players we've had in years." He sighed regretfully.

Ashley smothered a smile, well aware that her father was mourning not so much the loss of one player, but the probability that Gray McGraw's departure would lead to rather less blood on the ice. Not that McGraw was a particularly violent player, but he had a talent for making things happen.

"I vaguely remember," said Ashley, who never read the sports pages in spite of working in a store whose reason for existence was sport. "He had an accident, didn't he? Just over a year ago..."

"He sure did. I saw it on TV. McGraw was skating like a demon that night, but somehow he got shoved into the boards. It was sickening—you could hear his bones crack."

"Bones?" gulped Ashley faintly.

"Yes, his leg was broken in several places. That's why it took so long to heal."

"He doesn't walk with a limp, though," she objected.

"Oh, no. If he was in any other line of work he'd be just fine. But his leg will never be able to cope with the kind of punishment it would have to take if he kept on with his professional career. I read that he's been fighting it every inch of the way, determined to get back on the ice. But this story in the paper says he's finally been forced to give up." Toivo shook his head. "Must be pretty tough on a guy like that. He's always been a fighter, completely single-minded about what he wants. Won't keep him down, though. He's no whiner."

"No," muttered Ashley. "He's too busy throwing his weight about to whine. And he still has all that money—that must be some consolation."

"Besides, he's young," said Rosa dismissively. "He'll survive. Come on, you two, help me set this table before the rest of the gang comes home."

"Where are they all?" asked Ashley, taking in for the first time that the house was unusually quiet.

"Maria took them to a movie—except for Gina. She's playing next door with the Calders."

"Lovely." Ashley stretched. "Isn't it peaceful?" A moment later she wished she hadn't spoken, because, as soon as the words were out of her mouth, the back door burst open and five-year-old Gina's high treble shrieked gleefully, "Mom, Dad, I'm back!"

As if they could have failed to notice, thought her sister resignedly.

Two minutes after that the rest of the Kalani horde swarmed in, all shouting at once and anxious to tell anyone who would listen about the movie.

Ashley closed her eyes, as the headache that had been threatening all day burst forth in all its glory and began to pound nails inside her head. She must have been out of her mind earlier when she had been glad she still lived at home.

Sighing, she sat down at the table with the rest of her exuberant family. She loved them all dearly, of course, but sometimes it was impossible not to wish that they all lived somewhere else—a long way away—or that she did.

Ashley's one dream was to have a small, quiet home of her own, with roses and a picket fence—and no kids. Which was why she was working so hard to earn her honors degree in Commerce at Lakehead University—so that she could get a good job in the business world which would give her more than just enough to get by on. It was also why she still lived at home, at twenty-two the eldest of a family of seven. Her job at Boyko's paid for tuition, plus the small amount her parents would accept for room and board—and she knew that if she rented an apartment, even a shared one, it would take forever to realize her dream of roses and her own private peace. So she continued to live with her family, studying whenever and wherever it was possible, and somehow she managed to endure the constant noise.

Much later that evening, long after supper was over, Ashley sat in the room she shared with her sister Maria. She was humming under her breath and trailing a pen aimlessly across a page of clean white paper. The idea was to research an essay on Consumer Behavior. Unfortunately the only consumer she seemed able to concentrate on at the moment had thick dark hair, annoyingly seductive lips—and a thoroughly arrogant way of behaving.

With a groan of exasperation she gave up. Maria would be back from her date soon anyway. Listlessly she threw the pen down on her desk and started to get ready for bed.

Tomorrow would have to be a better day than this one.

As it turned out, not only tomorrow but the remainder of the week was better. The noise level at home stayed within tolerable bounds and she managed to get quite a lot of work done. It wasn't until the following Saturday that she found herself recalling that weekends at Boyko's could sometimes be even more trying than weekends spent at home with her family.

This fact was borne in on her forcibly when she looked up from a display of cold weather survival equipment she was arranging to see two ominous juvenile heads advancing side by side through the door.

Oh, dear! The Dalton twins. That meant trouble—double trouble. In flaming, redheaded spades.

She left the survival display half finished and went to stand by the cash register, from which vantage point she had a fairly comprehensive view of the shelves.

"Can I help you?" she called out, as Larry Dalton slouched by with his hands deep in his pockets.

"Nah, just looking," grunted Larry.

I'll bet, thought Ashley.

Len Dalton had disappeared behind a rack of skis, and she frowned, trying to remember what there was for him to get into back there.

It didn't take her long to find out. As she stared at the top of his ginger-colored head—all of him that was visible from this angle—suddenly both his hands appeared above the shelf. Between them he was balancing a barbell which was at least twenty pounds heavier than his twelve-year-old frame could support.

"Len, put that down at once," ordered Ashley.

She could have saved her breath. Even as she spoke, the barbell trembled precariously, wavered for a moment, then fell with an almighty crash onto the floor.

"Ow!" screeched Len. "Ow—ooch—ow! My foot—it's coming off! I'll sue!"

Ashley didn't pause to think twice. Placing one hand on the counter, she vaulted over it, landed lightly on both feet, and sped in the direction of Len's howls, which were increasing steadily in volume and beginning to sound like her idea of a banshee enjoying a night on the tiles. It wasn't until she was about to round the ski rack that it came to her that there was something else which wasn't quite as it should be. For one thing, Larry was nowhere in sight and was apparently totally oblivious to his brother's anguish. For another, just as her feet had swung over the top of the counter, she remembered encountering a pair of very dark eyes. They belonged to a man who had been entering the store at the moment the commotion had started. A man she had seen once before—and whom she most definitely did *not* want to see again.

Ashley stopped in her tracks, but only for a second. Len's howls had now reached heights that would have routed the most determined pack of wolves, and this was no time to worry about one out-of-work hockey player with the face of a seductive archangel and the disposition of an exceptionally ill-tempered toad.

She drew a deep breath to prepare herself for a probable scene of blood and mutilation, and stepped resolutely around the rack of skis.

Len Dalton sat on the floor with his head thrown back, and his mouth open wide to yell again. His legs were extended straight in front of him and the barbell lay five feet away against the wall.

Ashley's eyes narrowed as she glanced from the barbell to Len's apparently uninjured but exceedingly vociferous young form.

"What's the matter?" she asked sharply. And then, as he gave vent to another ear-splitting yell, "And you can stop that noise at once, Len Dalton!"

Len stopped, and two sullen blue eyes glanced up warily. "It fell," he told her, giving a creditable imitation of a whimper. "On my foot."

"Which one?"

"My—my left one," he pointed straight at his right big toe, which was protruding through a dirty white sneaker.

"Uh-huh," said Ashley. "Can you stand on it?"

"Nah, it's busted," he replied, relaxing visibly.

"Oh, dear." Slowly, with her eyes fixed innocently on the wall, Ashley put her hand on the nearest shelf and shook it, causing a stack of boxes to rock wildly back and forth above Len's head. "Oh dear," she said again, as a thirty-pound weight teetered dangerously, "I do hope it's not going to fall."

With another howl, genuine this time, Len shot up on to his feet and backed away.

"Hey, you watch it!" he shouted. "You'd just better..." His voice trailed off, as he saw that Ashley's mouth was pulled into a tight line, and that her normally friendly brown eyes had become anything but sympathetic slits.

"You, Len Dalton, had just better get out of this store," grated Ashley, who was fighting a very unprofessional urge to box a certain alleged customer's pointed ears. "Where's Larry?"

"Dunno," said Len, backing away again.

Larry's whereabouts did not remain a mystery for long.

Just as Ashley reached the counter, holding Len firmly by the arm, a wail went up from the back of the store that easily rivaled Len's Oscar-winning performance. It was followed by a youthful voice whining, "Hey, don't hit me, Mr. McGraw! I didn't mean to——"

"Don't lie to me," interrupted a cool male voice that Ashley suddenly realized was quite attractive. "If you do, I may lose my temper, in which case you'll get what you deserve."

The only response to that was a loud sniff, and a moment later Larry's small and reluctant figure was propelled around a shelf of camping supplies by a large and capable hand behind its shoulder. The hand marched him smartly up to the cash register to confront Ashley.

"It seems," said Gray dryly, "that between the two of us we've just foiled quite a neat little conspiracy."

"Weren't no con-conspiracy," said Larry, darting her a look that was pleading as well as resentful.

Ashley didn't answer, because she was having trouble dealing with the fact that, although Gray was the last person she had wanted to see again, the moment she heard his voice something inside her had done a backflip. And now that he was here, standing in front of her, all masculine and cool and in control, she found his presence altogether—stimulating? No—disturbing.

"Wh-what are you going to do with us, then?" asked Len, looking as if he might make a bolt for it.

Ashley tightened her grip on his arm, glanced questioningly at Gray, and finally managed to mumble, "I don't know. It all depends what you've done——"

"Didn't do nothing," the twins chanted in unison.

"Shut up," said Gray mildly, but in a tone that left no one in any doubt that he meant it.

They shut.

"As far as I can see," explained Gray, giving Ashley a faintly cynical smile, "these two had a clever little plot worked out. One of them would distract you by pretending he'd had an accident—that part went without a hitch—while the other one helped himself to two boxes of skates, a couple of down vests, and something that advertises itself as a high-protein energy food and looks like the sort of thing the dog keeps hiding under my bed."

"Protein bars," said Ashley automatically. "They're very good for you." Just now she felt much more comfortable discussing protein bars than anything remotely connected with his bed.

"I'll take your word for it," said Gray, who obviously didn't. "Meanwhile, what would you like to do with these two little gangsters? Before they're incarcerated permanently at your expense, which is no doubt what they're working up to."

"Not working up to nothin'," objected Larry, who didn't know what "incarcerated" meant.

"Shut up," said Gray. "Well, Ashley?"

So he remembered her name. He hadn't said anything to Mr. Boyko, though, or she'd have heard about it.

"I don't know," she said doubtfully. "Their mother's on welfare..."

"And they're on the road to ruin. All right, you two, we won't turn you in this time. Instead you'll go up to my place every Saturday till I say you can stop. You can do any chores I or my father want done, like shoveling snow, taking out the garbage, and walking the dog. Then you can do the same thing for our neighbors. They're both elderly. That should keep you out of stores on weekends for quite some time. And if I hear you've caused any kind of trouble at all," he glared at them, 'you'll wish I *had* turned you in to the police. Understand?"

They understood.

"Will we get paid?" asked Len unwisely, just before they opened the door.

"You'll get paid all right, where it hurts, if I hear any more nonsense from you," threatened Gray. But, as the two boys scuttled outside, he added on a more lenient note, "If you behave yourselves, I may give you a couple of skating lessons—if you're interested."

Just before the door closed with a resounding crash, Ashley saw two ginger heads turn in astonishment, as two pairs of eyes widened enthusiastically, and two young mouths parted in grins of delighted disbelief.

"That was nice of you," she said, not looking at him. "Thank you for your help, Mr. McGraw."

"Just protecting my property," replied Gray casually. "No need to thank me."

Ashley frowned and swung around to face him. "What did you say?" she asked, not understanding.

"I said I was protecting my property. This shop."

"But—but it's not your property. It's Mr. Boyko's."

"Not any more, it isn't," he replied equably. "Charlie Boyko signed the transfer papers this morning. As of three hours ago, all of Boyko's Sporting Goods Stores, plus one very large distributorship, belong lock, stock, barrel and..." his eyes glittered a challenge "...and Ashley Kalani, to me."

CHAPTER TWO

ASHLEY gaped at him, stunned. "What?" she asked stupidly. "But you can't..."

As Gray leaned back against the counter and folded his arms, the challenge in his eyes became quite blatant. She pushed a hair that wasn't there behind her ear, and went on with an effort to sound controlled, "I suppose you can. Buy out Boyko's, I mean——"

"I assure you, I have."

She swallowed. "Yes, but that certainly *doesn't* mean you own *me*. I don't come with the equipment and assets, Mr. McGraw."

He raised his eyebrows. "No? Charlie Boyko indicated that you did. On Fridays and Saturdays. And that a young man called Jack manages this outlet on weekdays."

"That's not the same as owning me. I work here, yes, but now that Mr. Boyko's sold the business——"

"Along with its assets."

Ashley clenched her teeth, an action which seemed to come naturally around Gray. "I told you I'm not an asset."

Gray smoothed a hand over his jaw. "Mmm," he murmured, "you may be right about that. But I'd like you to stay on just the same."

That did it. Ashley, who usually thought things over before she acted, opened her mouth and announced flatly, "I won't be able to do that, I'm afraid. Please accept my notice as of today."

Gray's face was a study. She could see that he was torn between surprise, indignation and, she strongly suspected, an urge to laugh that he was trying very hard not to betray.

She didn't wait to see which won out, but darted into the storeroom, seized her bag, then hurried back to the exit. Her fingers were already on the door when she felt a warm, masculine hand pressing her elbow.

"Don't run away," Gray's deep voice murmured in her ear. "I'm not really all that hard to get along with. Besides, Charlie Boyko is under the impression that you need the job."

"I don't need it that badly," she said, staring at a large, greasy palm print on the glass.

Quite gently, but very firmly, Gray swung her about to face him. "I've scared you off, haven't I?" he said quietly. "Perhaps that was was stupid of me. All the same, I definitely want you to stay."

"Why? And you didn't scare off." Her small chin jutted aggressively.

He shrugged, and she couldn't avoid noting the way his muscles flexed beneath his canary yellow sweatshirt. He was the sort of man who could wear rose pink and still look every inch male, she thought resentfully.

"All right, so I didn't scare you." He shrugged again, which only added to her confusion. "As a matter of fact, I want you to stay because one, I can use experienced help in my shops while I get on with the business of reorganizing head office. Two, you need a job, and three, it's damned unfair of you to leave me in the lurch when you were specifically included in the package." His eyes still glittered in a way that made her want to slap him.

"Mr. Boyko had no right to include me," snapped Ashley. "And why aren't you at head office now?"

"Where and why I choose to spend my time is my business, I think. And I expect Charlie thought he was doing you a favor."

"Some favor!" she scoffed. And then, less belligerently, "Maybe he did." It was possible. Mr. Boyko often did the unexpected. Although selling out without bothering to inform his staff was unusual even for him.

"Right. Then you'll stay." said Gray as if there were no more to be said. He put his hand on her arm and smiled disarmingly. "I'm sure we can manage to get along with each other if we put our minds to it."

When he looked at her like that, all warm and teasing and seductive, Ashley had a momentary feeling that she could get along with him all too well without putting much mind to it at all. She gave herself a quick mental shake. Gray's animal magnetism had nothing to do with anything. But her financial situation had. And she needed the money. There were other jobs in town, of course, but she'd start at a much lower salary and, satisfying as it would be to turn him down, she couldn't really afford the grand gesture.

"All right," she agreed grudgingly, "I'll stay for a trial period."

"Good. But that applies to you as well."

"What does?"

"The trial period. If I'm to be on trial, then so are you."

"Sounds fair," agreed Ashley, wishing she could tell him to take a hike. "And you can take your hand off my arm now, if you don't mind."

"Mmm?" He glanced down at the hand in question as if he had been wondering where he'd put it and was pleased to find it. Then he released her rather deliberately as the door swung open and a small group of customers shuffled in.

Ashley, grateful for the interruption and badly in need of something to keep her mind and eyes off Gray, swung immediately into action. By the time the customers left, she had succeeded in selling two pairs of skates, three complete ski outfits and a tent.

"Nice work." Gray, who had been standing behind a ski rack trying to look unobtrusive and not succeeding, clapped his hands together four times, very slowly, and strolled out onto the floor.

"What is?" asked Ashley, mystified.

"Your salesmanship. Or am I supposed to say salespersonship?"

"That *would* go against the grain, wouldn't it?" she jeered.

"Not really. I can get my tongue around it—just." He tilted his head to one side and gave her a long, contemplative stare. "And just as a matter of interest, do you always accept compliments so graciously?"

"Compliments?"

"That's what I said. I was complimenting you on your ability to move my merchandise. Or didn't you notice?"

His merchandise. Yes, it was his merchandise now, wasn't it? And of course she had noticed the compliment. It was just that, like everything else about this man, it had confused her—and it had been much easier to sneer than to smile sweetly.

"Thank you for the compliment, then," she said shortly. When Gray continued to look at her as if he were calculating her potential in fields far removed from sales, she added with a prim little grimace, "I took a course in sales management last year, so I certainly should be able to manage myself."

Yes, she should. But around him she wasn't convinced she could manage a duck pond, let alone a sales team—or a man.

"So you should," he agreed equably. "And that being the case, perhaps you'd care to manage me."

She swallowed. It wasn't possible. Hockey players were supposed to skate, not read minds.

"What do you mean?" she asked warily.

He pulled a badminton racket off a shelf and slapped it against his palm. "It may not have escaped your notice that I'm new to the world of commerce. People I can manage. They'll work for me as a team, or they'll find they don't work for me at all, so I don't foresee any problems on that score. But at the moment I happen to be interested in the day-to-day operation of my shops." His mouth curved up seductively. "So I'd like you to show me around—break me in gradually, so to speak."

"Break you...?" Ashley swallowed again, as visions which had very little to do with sporting goods ran deliciously through her mind. She pushed them away hastily. "Of course." She nodded, doing her best to look bored and businesslike. "It goes with my job, doesn't it?" When he continued to regard her with a small, irritating smile, she finished crossly, "What on earth made you *buy* a sporting goods company and settle in Thunder Bay, Mr. McGraw?"

Gray shrugged. "I decided I wanted to. Not that it has much to do with you, has it? However, there are—reasons why I need to be based here for the moment, and, as I'm familiar with certain aspects of sport, it seemed a reasonable option."

"Yes," said Ashley doubtfully, ignoring the gibe about her curiosity, and noting that his eyes were hooded now, the side of his face in shadow. "But surely you don't *have* to do anything? And you made the move awfully fast. There have been rumors that Mr. Boyko wanted to sell, of course, but he never said a word about it when he dropped in to check up on me last night."

"He didn't know." Gray's voice was curt. "And no, I don't 'have to do anything,' as you put it. But what did you expect? That I'd sit around on my backside drinking pink gins while I made love to anything passably attractive that happened to wander my way? That's what the papers say about me, isn't it?"

"No," said Ashley, surprised by the bitterness in his tone, and at the same time irritated by his bluntness. "They say you never keep still, even in your off hours, that you rarely drink because drink might put you off your game—and that you've had a great many girlfriends, none of whom has lasted very long. As to whether you made love to them . . ." She stopped, horrified by what she'd been about to say.

Gray grinned unpleasantly as another customer came through the door. "It's none of your business," he muttered out of the side of his mouth, "but since you were about to ask, no, I didn't always make love to them. Often there wasn't much time. Which may be why they rarely lasted long."

"I wasn't about to ask," hissed Ashley. The customer, smiling innocently, moved toward them. "And maybe they didn't last because they couldn't put up with your arrogance."

"Could be," he agreed nonchalantly.

She turned away to deal with the customer, and several others who followed, and it wasn't until half an hour later that she had an opportunity to wonder what had happened to her new boss.

She found him standing in the storeroom frowning at a pile of cash receipts. Deciding their previous conversation was better forgotten, she immediately went to work to explain them.

Ashley spent the rest of the afternoon, between customers, giving Gray a concise, practical and detailed description of the way a sporting goods shop was supposed to run. And every time she caught him looking at her with that maddening, assessing stare of his, she turned her back on him and went determinedly on about stock, invoices and the electronic vagaries of the cash register. But why, when he had just acquired a highly successful, multi-faceted enterprise, he should be hanging around this one small shop, she couldn't—or didn't want to— imagine.

By the end of the day, Gray was looking glazed as well as assessing, and Ashley was stifling a small thrill of triumph. It looked as though she might yet find a way to keep this man in his place! Except that this was his place, she realized with a sinking feeling.

At about four-thirty Mr. Boyko strode in, looking irritated. "Ah, there you are," he said to Gray accusingly. "Been looking for you. McGraw, you pushed this deal through like a tank brigade on the warpath, but we still have some details to iron out."

Ashley didn't listen to Gray's answer. She was thinking, half resentfully, that people like Gray McGraw, rich, famous, and used to getting what they wanted, probably didn't have to wait around for lawyers and due process like lesser mortals.

"We'll be in the back," Mr. Boyko said to her now. She nodded, and he hesitated and then added abruptly, "By the way, you've been a satisfactory employee, young lady. I've no doubt you'll do equally well with Mr. McGraw."

Ashley smiled weakly. "Um—yes," she mumbled. "Er—I'm sure... Um, yes."

Gray, who was casually flexing a weight with one hand, smiled cynically and said nothing.

A few minutes later she noticed it was well past closing time, so, leaving Mr. Boyko and Gray with their heads together at the small table in the back, she fetched her jacket and made her way quickly to the bus stop.

It was raining again, a cold, drizzling rain that gave promise of heavy snows to come. Ashley stood under the shelter and shivered. She should have worn a coat instead of this inadequate jacket, but winter was late this year—and anyway, Maria had borrowed her coat.

Twenty minutes later she was still shivering as she glanced at her watch and wondered what had happened to the bus. She was the only one waiting. Oh, dear, she thought disgustedly, this *was* the end of a perfect day. First the Dalton twins, then *that man* taking over Mr. Boyko's business—and now the bus was late. Naturally it was raining.

Glumly her thoughts strayed to the weeks ahead. How in the world was she going to survive working for Gray McGraw? Oh, certainly he'd been swift, effective and— she had to admit it—even kind, in dealing with the terrible twosome. But she couldn't see much else in his favor. He was easy to look at all right, but he seemed to know it, and if he was going to go on as he'd begun, alternately biting her head off, and virtually propositioning her with his eyes, she didn't think she'd able to stand it. Except that perhaps, if she were lucky, he might spend most of his time at head office—or intimidating staff at his other shops...

She pulled her collar up over her ears and hunched down into her jacket.

"Need a lift?"

Ashley jumped, and hit her shin on the bench that was much too wet to sit on. Oh, no! It couldn't be. She'd heard quite enough of that voice for one day.

But of course it was.

"No, thank you," she said frigidly. "The bus will be along in just a minute."

"It won't, you know. There's been a breakdown. And if you're worrying because your mother told you not to accept lifts from strangers, I promise you I'm really quite harmless.''

"I doubt that," said Ashley, before she could stop herself. When she looked up, he was smiling that slow, predatory smile again—the one that had so unnerved her from the first.

"Do you, now?" he said softly. "How very flattering!"

"It wasn't meant to be a compliment," snapped Ashley.

"No, I didn't think it was. Now, do you intend to stand there in the cold waiting for a bus that isn't coming, or are you going to act like the intelligent young woman I hope you are, and get in?"

He's making sense, she thought despairingly. Damn him, he's making sense! But does he *have* to be so damn patronizing about it?

Yes, she answered herself, of course he does. He's spent a lifetime being superior to everyone else.

"Thank you," she said stiffly, bowing to the inevitable. "It's very kind of you."

"No, it isn't. I'm just looking after my investment. Employees who catch pneumonia from standing around in the rain aren't much use to me."

Ashley pursed her lips and said nothing as he pushed open the door of a long, low, sexy white car, then watched interestedly as she climbed in and began to struggle vainly with the seat belt.

"For crying out loud, we'll be here all night," he muttered, when her efforts met with no success whatever. "Here, let me do it."

She drew in her breath sharply as his capable hand brushed against her thigh.

Gray, noticing, smiled in a way that reminded her of a very competent tiger on the prowl.

"Why can't you have seat belts like other people's?" she demanded grumpily.

"I have. Other people can do them up. Why are you so clumsy?"

"I'm not..." She stopped. He was right. She'd always been useless when it came to fastening things, opening jars, or hammering nails in straight. "I guess I am," she admitted reluctantly, "but you're not much of a gentleman to say so."

"At least you've got that right," he said grimly.

Ashley sighed. "I thought we were going to try to get along," she reminded him.

"We were. And I'm glad you said that." He began to back the car away from the curb.

"Why?"

"Because, if I'd had to put up with any more of your bad temper, I'd have been sorely tempted to throw you out on the road."

"I'm not bad-tempered," she protested.

"No? Then if this is your normal disposition, remind me to avoid you when you're mad."

"It's all your fault if I'm grumpy," she retorted, frowning irritably out at the rain.

"I fail to see why."

"Because you're such a patronizing, self-satisfied jerk!" she retorted without thinking. "I'm not one of your adoring fans, you know."

Gray rested one arm along the back of the seat and curled his fingers in her hair, tugging it so that she had to turn to face him. "Yes, I *had* noticed. But if you despise the sporting world so much, what are you doing working in the business?" he inquired, in a voice that sounded as though it meant to have an answer.

"You asked me to stay. And I've worked at Boyko's for ages. Besides," she added, with reluctant honesty, "I don't really despise the sporting world. I'm just not that interested. And I *have* met too many sports people who think they're God's gift to the rest of us."

"Including me."

It wasn't a question, it was a statement. He was still twisting her hair so she couldn't look away, and she saw that his strong profile had gone all flintlike and hard. So had his voice—and suddenly she wasn't sure whether she'd meant to include him in her blanket condemnation of sports types or not. At this moment she wasn't sure of anything. Especially him.

"I don't know," she hedged. "I don't know you well enough."

"Sure you do," he said flatly. "You read the papers, don't you?"

"Yes, but I don't always believe them."

"Hmm, how refreshing! You surprise me sometimes, Ms. K."

To Ashley's own surprise, he sounded almost friendly now, casual and even approving. She decided to take advantage of this lighter mood, and said quickly, "That's nice. And now do you think you could put your hands where they belong—instead of in my hair, Mr. McGraw?"

"Certainly." He removed his hand at once and gripped the wheel. "And do you think you could manage to call me Gray if I call you Ashley?"

"But I always called Mr. Boyko by his last name——"

"Did you? But I'm not Mr. Boyko—or hadn't you noticed?" He swiveled around suddenly and gave her a wide, deliberately suggestive grin. "Perhaps you'd like me to prove it to you, Ashley."

"No, thank you," she said quickly, wishing her whole body wasn't going limp with... Oh, no. No, no, no. *Not* with desire. She'd had plenty of casual boyfriends in her time, and she had never had trouble holding them at bay. She was *not* going to fall violently in lust with an egocentric hunk like Gray McGraw. It was against her principles.

"That's too bad. You don't know what you're missing," Gray was drawling. His eyes were fixed on the road, but she had no need to see them. She knew they were laughing at her, so she lifted her chin haughtily and didn't answer.

A few minutes later, as they pulled up in front of her parents' house in Fort William, Gray said abruptly, "Well?"

"Well what?" She blinked.

"Will you kindly stop calling me Mr. McGraw?"

Oh, anything for a quiet life, thought Ashley, who could think of several imprudent things she'd like to call him. "Of course," she said coolly. "You're the boss."

"I'm glad you've remembered that." His tone was mild, without noticeable inflection, but those improbable eyes as he turned to look at her were almost black, and they glinted with something she couldn't even pretend to understand. Even the faint menace in his words left her with a persistent feeling that behind the menace lay something else—something that might not be threatening after all.

She gave up. "Thank you for the ride, Mr.—Gray," she said quickly.

"My pleasure."

"Was it?" She paused as he came around to help her out, then asked suspiciously, "How did you know where I lived?"

"Personnel records. You came with the business, remember?"

As Ashley glared at him, he moved away from her, swung himself into the car, and raised one arm in a careless farewell salute.

"Good night, Ashley. Thank you for not deserting the sinking ship."

She gaped at him, and a moment later she was standing alone on the pavement.

Now what did he mean by that? Boyko's Sporting Goods most certainly wasn't sinking. In fact it was doing phenomenally well. So was he referring to himself? His star was undoubtedly on the wane in the sports world, but that didn't appear to be sinking him at all. On the contrary, as far as she could see, the reversal in his fortunes had, if anything, only served to make him more autocratic and in command of himself than ever. In fact he seemed to have the odd idea that he was also in command of her. Well, he had another think coming on that point. She kicked restlessly at a loose stone on the pavement, discovered she was getting wetter by the minute, and hurried up the path to the door.

The moment she opened it, she almost wished she was back in Gray's car. Wonderful smells were coming from the kitchen, but that was the only positive note in an appalling cacophony of negatives. And cacophony was the operative word.

At the top of the squeaking turn-of-the-century stairs, Maria was shouting at some unseen sibling to hurry up and get out of the bathroom because she had a date after supper. The unseen sibling, whose voice Ashley didn't need to hear because it was bound to belong to her sister Sophia, was yelling something ribald in response. At the bottom of the stairs, Gina was in tears over a childhood tragedy, and eleven-year-old Nick was telling her, loudly, to dry up.

That's four of them, thought Ashley tiredly. Two to go.

She wasn't disappointed. Behind her the door burst open and Rocky and Carlo exploded into the narrow hallway, almost knocking her over.

"Sorry, Ash," shouted Rocky. "Got to run. Come on, Carlo!"

At that moment Rosa, waving a wooden spoon, stormed out of the kitchen and shouted at them all to be quiet. For about thirty seconds there was blessed peace, then Gina said, "Pig!" to Nick, and all was bedlam again.

Ashley groaned and ran up the stairs to her bedroom, now occupied by an explosively indignant Maria.

"Sophia's a bitch!" she was exclaiming. "She knows Bill's coming for me as soon as supper's over."

"Yes, but I think Rod's coming for her," said Ashley, wishing the Pied Piper would come for the lot of them, and the sooner the better. Why did she have to be the only member of this family who put any premium on quiet? Usually, of course, she managed to endure the racket with a fixed smile and stoical indifference. But it was harder than usual tonight. She'd had an exceptionally trying day herself.

By the time she stumbled into bed, Ashley felt like a very limp dishrag that was about to be consigned to the dustbin.

She awoke the next morning to more noise, and the memory that her nice, secure job was no longer secure. Of course Gray had said she could keep it—but that was the whole point. *He* was at the root of her insecurity. She sighed, turned over, tried to get some more sleep, and ten minutes later gave up.

She spent the rest of the day trying to study, never an easy task in her household, but her mind just wouldn't stay in gear.

When the phone rang for her at three o'clock, she picked it up with a feeling of relief. Maybe one of her friends was going to ask her out, so that she could escape from this unproductive madhouse.

Her relief didn't last long. Someone *was* asking her out. But it wasn't one of her friends.

It was Gray McGraw.

CHAPTER THREE

"WHAT did you say?" Ashley murmured into the mouthpiece. "I don't think..."

"I said will you have dinner with me tonight?" Gray repeated.

"Oh. But why?"

She heard a faint sigh of exasperation. "It's usual to reply, 'Thank you, I'd like to,' or 'No, thank you,' followed by an excuse."

"No, thank you," she said quickly.

"Well?"

"Well what?" Hadn't they been this route before?

"What's your excuse?"

"Do I have to have one?"

"If you don't want me to arrive on your doorstep in ten minutes, it would be advisable." He spoke lightly, but with an undertone that convinced her he meant it.

"No, don't do that," she said with more haste than good manners. "Er—I'm busy tonight."

"Are you, now? Doing what?"

"Is it any of your business?"

"I think so. Because I don't believe you're busy at all," he said flatly. "You *are* scared of me, aren't you, Ashley Kalani?"

"Of course I'm not! It's just——" Her words were cut off as a piercing scream came from the living room and Carlo dashed out into the hall with a demonic grin on his face. He was holding Gina's favorite battered doll above his head, and a screeching Gina was charging in hot pursuit.

Oh, Lord, thought Ashley. Perhaps, after all, dinner with Gray McGraw would be preferable to another impossible evening with her family—which from the look of things was what was shaping up. And of *course* she wasn't scared of him. That was ridiculous.

"All right," she muttered. "Thank you, I'd like to come."

"That's better. I'll be over at six o'clock. Oh, and by the way, you have nothing to worry about. This is strictly a business engagement."

"Oh, is that all?" said Ashley, trying to keep the relief out of her voice, and then wondering why relief was followed by an annoying stab of disappointment.

"Of course it's all. I'll see you at six."

It was only after she'd hung up the phone that it occurred to Ashley to wonder just what kind of business he had in mind.

She told her mother she wouldn't be home that evening and then went back upstairs to make a critical decision about clothes. Pants would be too casual, her red special-occasion dress too revealing. That left the neat navy blue number she'd bought for possible interviews, or an equally neat skirt and blouse. Obviously the skirt and blouse would have to do. Her budget being what it wasn't, she rarely spent anything on clothes.

Half an hour later, after changing into a black wool skirt with a high-necked, full-sleeved white blouse, she sat down again to get on with her studies. Fifteen minutes after that she realized that instead of studying organizational behavior and social marketing she was contemplating the organizational behavior of her new boss—who had successfully organized her into going out with him. Why on earth had she agreed? She didn't even like the man, she didn't really believe he meant to discuss any legitimate kind of business and, contrary to what she had told him—and herself—she was *dead* scared of him.

Oh, she didn't think he'd beat her up or anything. But there was something dangerously magnetic about him, something seductive and sensuous that attracted her as much as it repelled her. She didn't want to be drawn into his orbit, to become one of the conquests he hadn't had time to make love to...

Oh, Lord! What was she thinking of? She had always been so careful not to let any of her boyfriends get serious, because there was no room in her life for that kind of involvement. So how could she even think about making love to Gray? Her dream was of a good job and her own private space, and she couldn't afford to let romantic distractions interfere with the goal in any way. Not now. Maybe not ever.

She ran her fingers through her hair, and reflected vaguely that it was time she got it cut.

No, of course she didn't want to make love to Gray. He was brusque to the point of rudeness half the time, and incredibly overbearing. Apart from which, she was too old to go falling for a man just because he had a beautiful male body and a full-lipped, arrogant smile. Much too old. So all she needed at the moment was for him to take her somewhere quiet, where she could eat a leisurely meal uninterrupted by tribal warfare over who had the largest helping of ice cream or the least spinach.

By the time Gray arrived—at five minutes past six and looking quite magnificently male in an impeccably cut dark suit with a wine red tie—she was was able to greet him with a cool smile and a firm handshake. He curled his fingers around her palm as his eyes warmly approved her demure but attractive outfit, and immediately, as Ashley had known they would, Sophia and Maria burst out of the living room and slid to an abrupt halt in front of the stairs.

She tried to withdraw her hand, but Gray only tightened his grip as a slow smile canted the corner of his mouth.

"Your sisters?" he inquired softly, nodding at the two dark-haired girls.

"Yes. Yes, Maria and Sophia—this is Gray."

"We know," breathed Maria, looking starstruck.

Sophia, even more forthright, gave him an approving grin and said cheerfully, "Hi! We've read a whole lot about *you*. It's about time Ashley had a boyfriend."

"Sophia!" groaned Ashley, blushing to the soles of her feet. "Gray is just my boss, not my boyfriend."

"The two are not mutually exclusive," drawled Gray, who was still holding on to her hand and watching her with that maddening little grin.

"Yes, they are," said Ashley, trying desperately to pull away from him. "Can we go? Now?"

"Say please."

"Please," she ground out through barely parted lips.

"Good girl. Where's your coat?"

Finally, to her enormous relief, he released her and allowed her to drag her coat from the cupboard. As he helped her on with it his fingers lingered for a moment on her shoulders and then he pulled her arm through his to march her out of the door with almost military briskness.

Behind them Ashley heard Maria and Sophia break into hysterical giggles.

"So you don't have a boyfriend?" mused Gray. Once again his hand was brushing her thigh as he fastened her seat belt.

"No," said Ashley shortly.

He was still bent toward her, and his eyes glittered very close to her own. "How does that happen? Pigheadedness, bad manners—or bad management?"

"Luck," said Ashley viciously, reaching for the handle of the door. She'd had enough of his mockery.

Gray's lips twitched. "Not so fast!" His hand closed over her fist. "Where do you think you're going, little lady?"

"Home."

"Oh, no, you're not." As she gaped up at him, he put one arm firmly around her shoulder, dragging her against him, and the other on the wheel of the car.

"What are you doing?" she protested.

"Not what I'd like to be doing at this moment," he assured her, starting the engine. "You try me sorely sometimes, Ms. Kalani. However, as what I have in mind is probably illegal, all I'm doing is taking you out for a meal."

"But you can't——"

"I can, you know."

Yes, he could. He was. What was it her father had said about Gray's being completely single-minded about what he wanted? Bloody-minded, more likely. There wasn't any special reason why he should want her company—strictly on a business basis, of course. No reason at all.

For the remainder of the drive to the old house which had been converted to an elegant restaurant, Ashley maintained a stiffly pointed silence. The only problem was that every time she glanced up at Gray's profile, she detected that aggravating little cant to his lips, and she had a disconcerting feeling that he was thoroughly enjoying her pointed silence. She scowled. He really was the most impossible man!

Happily, by the time they had been shown to a blessedly quiet corner by an attentive staff, and Gray had ordered some excellent champagne, she had begun to mellow a little. It was nice here in the softly lit restaurant with the dark paneling and atmosphere of restrained and restful luxury. And Gray was a very attractive man. He was also smiling that sexy smile again. But more importantly, he was taking her away from all the noise and clamor of her home.

"So," he said, raising his glass to her, "dare I drink to a pleasant evening?"

She had a feeling he was patronizing her again, but he looked horribly impressive this evening, and it was hard to withstand the aura of power and raw sexuality he exuded quite naturally, and without apparent effort. The thought of an *unpleasant* evening in his company made her shiver, so she raised her own glass and said lightly, "I don't see why not. We should be able to get along for a couple of hours."

"Mmm," Gray nodded, "we should. And if you behave yourself, we will. Incidentally, you look wonderful when you're angry, my dear—which seems to be most of the time. But you're even more ravishing when you smile."

He was teasing her, she supposed, but she wasn't at all sure she liked it.

"Behaving oneself is so boring," she said, attempting to sound sophisticated and at the same time put him in his place. "By the way, I'm not at all susceptible to flattery. I was always called Pixie-face at school, and I'm much too small and skinny to be ravishing."

She thought she heard him mutter something under his breath which sounded like, "But not to be ravished." Then he raised his voice and said pensively, "I like pixies. Especially pixies who misbehave." His dark gaze raked over her with suggestive innuendo, and she was horrified to feel a warm curl of excitement stir in her stomach.

"I didn't mean——" she began uncomfortably.

"I was afraid you didn't. Ah, well, that being the case, I'll do my best to keep you in line."

"I've no intention of being kept in line," retorted Ashley. "And I wish you'd stop tying me in knots." She took a deep breath. "What was the business you wanted to talk about, Mr. McGraw?"

"Ah, I'm Mr. McGraw again, am I? I suppose you might call it the business of mending fences."

She blinked. "What?"

Gray picked up his glass again and studied its pale contents reflectively. "You and I got off on the wrong foot," he explained. "As I prefer to have my staff work *with* me rather than against me, I'm softening you up with a good dinner in the hopes that we can have a satisfactory working relationship without getting on each other's nerves more than—oh, say once or twice a week. You're good at your job, Ashley. I don't mean to lose you."

So that was what this was all about. Irritatingly, once again she felt that stab of disappointment. "You won't lose me," she assured him, smiling too brightly. "I do need the job, as you well know."

"Mmm, that brings me to another point. Any chance of enlisting your services on weekdays?"

Ashley shook her head quickly. "No, I'm sorry, but I'm in my last year of college and I really can't afford the extra time."

"Fair enough." He nodded, and leaned back in his chair, his dark eyes resting thoughtfully on her face. "What do you plan to do when you're finished with your studies, Ashley?"

He seemed to have stopped baiting her for the time being, and, as he looked as though he might be genuinely interested, she told him. When their meal came— Gray had been right about good food softening her up— she continued to talk about her dreams of a quiet home of her own. She even let slip the fact that, much as she loved her family, she really couldn't wait to get away.

"You could marry away," he suggested with a bland and overly innocent smile.

"Oh, no, I couldn't. *I'm* not stepping out of the frying pan into the fire—not for any man!"

"Hmm." He raised his eyebrows. "Is that how you view marriage? As a fire? How very promising for that husband you're not going to have!"

Ashley stared at him, not sure how to handle this sudden switch from polite listener to mocking wolf on the make. All the same, his words served to remind her of the kind of man she was with, and also that she'd been talking about herself for the better part of an hour. 'I talk too much," she said frigidly. "What about you?"

"Do *I* talk too much?"

She sighed heavily. "I meant I've been telling you all about my plans. Now it's your turn."

"Hmm." He strummed his fingers on the edge of the table. "By any chance, did you just remember that your mother told you you're supposed to flatter men's egos by getting them to talk about themselves?"

"My mother doesn't believe in egos. And, of all the men I've met, I'd say you have the ego that's least in need of a boost."

"You *are* good for the soul! I suppose you believe in hair shirts and flagellation too."

"No, just in pricking balloons."

"Ouch!" He winced, then murmured reflectively, 'Ah, well, I suppose there's a first time for everything."

She frowned. "Such as?"

"Such as being compared to a balloon."

Ashley stared across the table at his lean, supple body and muscular neck, saw the way the pale cream shirt clung to his imposing frame, imagined long legs stretched out underneath the table—and then, to her own amazement as much as his, she burst out laughing.

"I'm sorry," she muttered a few minutes later, as Gray raised an eloquently resigned eyebrow. "You're quite right. I can't think of anyone less like a balloon than you are."

"Hmm. And what's that supposed to mean?" he growled. "That I'm underweight?"

"No. It was a compliment." Why did she feel shy all of a sudden?

"We *are* coming along, aren't we?" he gibed. "I didn't think you knew what the word meant."

This was getting ridiculous. Gray was obviously having a wonderful time at her expense, and she, like a fool, was making it easy for him. Well, she wasn't going to do it any longer. This conversation was going to be returned smartly to the realm of polite and casual sociability.

"Of course I know what it means," she said, purposely misunderstanding him. "Now please do tell me about yourself." She felt a bit like a psychiatrist with a particularly tricky patient. "What about your family?"

To her surprise, his eyes seemed to darken. But that wasn't possible, was it? They were already darker than midnight.

"My mother's dead," he said briefly. When he saw her open her mouth to express sympathy, he added roughly, "She died a few months after I was born. I have no brothers or sisters."

Ashley stifled an inexcusable urge to say, "You're lucky," and said, "Oh, how sad," instead.

He shrugged. "Yes."

Oh, dear. If she'd paid attention to sports, she'd have known all that. But now her attempt to bring their conversation into less loaded channels had apparently backfired. Gray's body had gone disconcertingly rigid, to the point where he reminded her of nothing so much as some brooding, primitive statue. The kind that turned up in museums glowering down at marble floors—and tourists more interested in lunch than history.

Ashley tried again. "Your father's still in Thunder Bay, isn't he?" she asked brightly. "I remember my dad saying how proud he was of you, how terribly dedicated to your career——"

"Yes, he's still here."

The words were harsh, bitten off, and she supposed she'd put her foot in it again. But it wasn't her fault, and she resented his abruptness.

"I'm sorry," she said coolly, "I didn't think. Of course it must be heartbreaking for him now that you're not able to play."

He didn't answer, and his eyes reflected an intent, bitterly ironic cynicism. "But of course it's much worse for you," she added reluctantly.

"What makes you think so?"

"Well, I—I don't know, but it's all you've ever done, and you were so good at it..."

"That doesn't mean I'm no good at anything else." His words sliced the air with a cold violence that shocked her.

"No, of course it doesn't——"

"And don't sit there feeling sorry for me!"

"Why not?" she asked, goaded. "You feel sorry for yourself, don't you?"

Oh, Lord, what had made her say that? He had good reason to resent the blow that fate had dealt him.

He was leaning toward her now, one closed fist resting on the table. "No," he said quietly—too quietly, "I don't."

"Oh. Then——"

"Self-pity is an unattractive emotion. I don't need your sympathy, Ashley."

He wasn't going to get it either. Sympathy was not her uppermost emotion at this moment. It might have been—almost had been. But Gray's behavior over the last few minutes had made her want to slap him—hard—not heap unwanted compassion on his head. When she found she was sitting on her hands in order to prevent herself from doing just that, she stood up.

"Thank you for a nice dinner," she said formally, "but I think I've outstayed my welcome."

"Sit down." Gray put out his hand and caught her by the wrist.

Ashley swallowed, tried to pull away—and saw something in his eyes that made her hesitate.

She sat.

Gray, smiling grimly, released her arm.

"Why do you want me to stay?" she asked, knowing she sounded sulky, but not knowing what to do about it. She *felt* sulky—or resentful anyway. She had asked some perfectly innocent questions about his family, more to make conversation than from curiosity, and he had reacted like an unpredictable bear.

"Because you interest me," he replied bluntly.

"Oh. Well, you're beginning not to interest me at all, I'm afraid. You're much too bossy for my taste." When his eyes glittered a challenge that might have been a threat, she shrugged. "All right, I take it back, then."

She didn't, but she was tired of this conversation.

"Do you?" He studied her face with a curious concentration, then ran his hands through his hair and half smiled. "Perhaps you shouldn't. I'm told there was a time, shortly after the accident, when I made life hell for everyone who came near me."

Ashley choked back an impulse to remark that things hadn't changed much, then, had they? Because now, contrarily, she did feel an unwilling sympathy for this difficult man, in spite of all his rough edges.

"That's understandable," she said quietly.

"Is it?" he said dismissively. "I'm glad you think so."

She stared at him, frowning. What was it about Gray McGraw that kept her almost permanently on edge? There was an abrasive bitterness about him sometimes that seemed to be directed not so much at life, or at himself, but at her. And yet at other times he actually seemed to like her. It didn't make sense.

She looked him straight in the eye. "I do think so," he said. "Of course it was hard to accept that your career was over."

His mouth twisted. "Not that hard. It wasn't the first battle I'd lost. I've had other setbacks." He lifted his shoulders, then seemed to relax slightly. "Besides, I've never seen the point of postmortems unless they could be the start of something better. Which was why, after a particularly inexcusable episode of shouting at two doctors, my father and an unfortunate passing nurse, I realized I had to come to terms with the fact that it was time I moved on to greener fields. Preferably with a good grace."

"So you did?"

"More or less."

"Sometimes less," Ashley observed dryly.

To her surprise, he gave her a smoldering, decidedly attractive smile. "I can't deny it. You bring out the worst in me, Ashley."

"In that case why did you ask me out to dinner?"

"I'd have thought that was obvious." The smile stopped smoldering and turned into what she supposed was meant to be a leer.

"Are you suggesting what I think you're suggesting?" she demanded.

"Nope. Just seeing if I can make your eyes flash. I told you, I only wanted to talk business."

"There are lots of different kinds of business," she reminded him, still suspicious.

"Well, I'm always open to suggestions..."

"Oh, stop it!" she snapped, wondering why she always got the worst of it when she attempted a war of words with Gray. At the same time, she was obliged to squelch a maddening desire to laugh.

"And you stop behaving as if you think I'm about to assault you. I promise you, the owners wouldn't allow it."

"Maybe not, but there's always afterward," she pointed out.

"Mmm. And as I said, I'm always open to suggestions. Now drink your coffee."

Ashley gave up. She delivered a frosty glare across the table and swallowed the brew in one gulp.

"That's what I like to see," said Gray approvingly. "A woman who does what she's told. Shall we go?"

It was on the tip of her tongue to tell him *he* could go, but she recalled in time that buses were few and far between at this time of night, and that the restaurant was a long way from home.

Pointing her nose at an improbable angle, she stood up and marched across to the coat check without bothering to see if he was behind her.

He was. She was made aware of that quite forcibly when she felt the pressure of his thigh along her hip, and found he had taken her coat and was easing it over her shoulders. The heated shudder that went through her at that moment told her, as nothing else could have done, that, whatever she might feel about Gray's personality, she was anything but immune to the impact of his physical presence.

She pulled away from him hastily, then was chagrined to see that his mouth had curled up in an amused, much too knowing grin.

Later, when she saw him reach for her seat belt, desperation enabled her to master it herself—which didn't help at all, because the grin became a shout of outright laughter.

"Are we going to drive home in outraged silence?" he asked interestedly, when Ashley's nose showed no signs of descending.

"Of course not," she replied frigidly. "Why should we?"

"Ah," he nodded, "not outraged silence. Icy uninterest—I see. You'd have made a good duchess, my dear. The old-fashioned kind who believed in keeping the riffraff in their place."

To her consternation, Ashley discovered she was again fighting that irritating urge to laugh. After a while she gave in to it. Apparently she wasn't the only one who was good at pricking balloons.

"That's better," said Gray. "Much better. Dare I assume I'm forgiven, then? Not that I can recall doing anything unusually obnoxious."

"You haven't really," sighed Ashley. "Except give me dinner and drive me to contemplate murder."

"Is that so? Mine, I presume?"

"Naturally." She darted a look at him and saw that, as she had suspected, his smile was as broad as it was complacent.

But it wasn't complacency she observed when they drew up in front of her house a short time later. Even in the dim glow of the streetlight, she could see that the glint in his eyes meant retribution.

It wasn't an angry retribution, though. As he stretched his arm along the back of the seat, the purposeful look he directed at her spoke more of amusement than indignation. Nonetheless, she had no doubt whatever that it meant trouble. For her.

"Thank you," she mumbled quickly. "Thank you very much. It's been a—a nice evening. Perhaps I'll see you on Friday, then. No, I suppose not. At work, I mean——"

"Stop babbling! The evening isn't over yet. We have some unfinished business to attend to."

"No, we haven't. It's late——"

His fingers were stroking her neck, sending searing shivers down her spine. His thigh was pressing against her leg and his free hand was turning her face toward his...

"I—what—don't..." she gasped, made incoherent by the feel and scent of him, by his closeness, and by the new and unwanted sensations that were surging through her like blue-pointed flames.

"Don't what?" he murmured caressingly.

"Don't—don't..."

"Don't kiss you? But you want me to, don't you?" He unfastened the top button of her coat.

"No—I..." She gave a little groan. "No, Gray."

"Are you sure?"

Two other buttons opened and his hand slipped beneath the coat, moving down to curve around the soft wool covering her hip—and she groaned again.

"You'll have to kiss *me*, then, won't you?" he said softly. "If you want to be kissed, that is."

Oh, yes, she did want to be kissed, quite desperately, but this was all wrong. Gray was her boss, a man she didn't much like, a man who believed in love 'em—when you had the time—and leave 'em. He had more or less said so.

She mustn't kiss him. She mustn't. But his lips were almost touching her cheek now, the fingers at her neck were beneath her collar, and that other hand—it was doing intoxicating, unbelievably wonderful things to her hip, to her lower back—and down farther...

She made a small sound, saw his eyes gleaming in the darkness, and with a shiver of undeniable desire turned her lips expectantly to his.

CHAPTER FOUR

HE TASTED of wine, warm and aromatic, and Ashley's mouth clung desperately to his, held there by a need she had never suspected she could feel.

Gray let her make the first tentative exploration, running her tongue across his lips while he stayed quite still, his hands not moving now as they rested on her hip and beside her neck. But when, unable to bear his lack of response, she pressed herself against him and wrapped her arms fiercely around his neck, he gave a low, triumphant growl and pulled her up tightly against his chest.

Then he kissed her, very thoroughly, assaulting her mouth until her lips parted willingly and her lungs were completely emptied of breath. After that, apparently deciding his unfinished business had been satisfactorily taken care of, he held her away from him and said with shattering control, "Well, that's that, then."

Ashley, still fighting to get her breath back, stared at him disbelievingly, until at last she was able to gasp out, "What——? You bastard! Why—why did you do that?"

"I didn't. You did."

"But you made me!"

"Did I? In that case, perhaps I did it because I wanted to. Or maybe I only wanted to see if I could. Take your choice."

"Bastard!" she repeated.

"Why? Because you kissed me?"

"I didn't——"

"Yes, you did, and very nice it was too. I thought it might be."

"Oh!" exclaimed Ashley. "Oh, you—you—how *could* you?" She scrabbled frantically for the handle of the door, found it, and stumbled out onto the cold gray street.

"Hey," said Gray, leaning across the seat to laugh up at her, "it wasn't that bad, was it?"

"Yes, it was," she snapped, glaring into his mocking, upturned face. "It was..."

Oh, hell! The truth was, it hadn't been bad at all. It had been sensational. But when he looked at her as he was now, all predatory and confident and teasing, she was still hard put to it not to punch him on his arrogant nose—although, from the looks of it, it had received worse damage in its time than any she would be likely to inflict.

"Never mind," she said, turning away from him to stare gloomily up at the sky. "It was only a kiss."

"Thank you for the accolade," Gray said dryly.

"Don't mention it. Good night." Ashley's head was still tilted to the heavens, and the moment the words were out of her mouth she felt something cold and wet land softly on the top of her nose.

The first snowflake. She brushed it away hurriedly, and marched up the path to her door.

Behind her, as she put the key in the lock, she could have sworn she heard the sound of Gray's laughter ringing out warm and full-throated on the winter air.

Damn it, the man has an attractive laugh, she thought irritably, as she shut the door behind her and stepped into the mercifully quiet hall. And it wasn't only his laugh that was attractive. No wonder the less reputable papers had wasted so much newsprint speculating on the details of his love life! She kicked off her shoes and bent to pick them up wearily. This whole episode was going to be very awkward. She wanted to keep her job, but she didn't know if she could continue to work for Gray unless he kept out of her way—as it would be easy enough for him to do if he chose. The trouble was, after tonight, she had an uncomfortable feeling he wouldn't choose.

Oh, he wasn't all bad, of course, she mused grudgingly as she trudged up the stairs. He had an unpredictable temper, an annoying habit of laughing at her, and he was probably all too well aware of the effect he had on unwary women like herself. But he had been nice about the Dalton twins, and once or twice this evening she thought she had detected a certain vulnerability beneath the glossy surface. Something that perhaps went deeper than a natural resentment at being forced to give up the life he loved—which would have ended in a few years anyway.

She sighed as she pushed open the bedroom door, thinking that maybe there was a reason for Gray's behavior. She didn't understand it, and she didn't like it, but she might have to learn to live with it—because there was no question that she needed the job. Assuming she still had it, of course, and somehow, whatever else he might be, she didn't think Gray was a man who would go back on a promise. She sighed again. If only he weren't so damned unsettling! If only he hadn't kissed her . . .

That night she fell asleep trying not to think about that kiss. It had been unlike any she had ever given or received in the past. Those other kisses had been sweet and casual, more experimental than passionate. But Gray's kiss had been quite different—and she must make sure that it didn't happen again. Even if it would do her any good to fall head over heels for Thunder Bay's famous son, which she doubted, she hadn't time for entanglements of that nature . . . She really hadn't . . .

Maria snored gently, and Ashley's eyes closed. A moment after that she was fast asleep.

When she awoke the next morning, the ground was covered with thick white folds of snow.

It continued to snow intermittently all week, and there was a fresh fall on Friday morning, so that when she left the university to go to work that evening the trees were all covered with white lace, and the grass was a clean, shining blanket. Normally it wouldn't be busy at Boyko's on a night like this, but Christmas was coming soon, so you never knew...

All week she had half expected Gray to call, either to demand that she go out with him again or else to tell her she didn't have a job. She had resolved to say no to the former, and to maintain a dignified unconcern if he should fire her.

But he hadn't called, and it was with a faint feeling of trepidation that she pushed open the door of the store at five to five.

There was no sign of Gray. Not that there was any reason for him to be here, she assured herself. Jack, the young man who managed the store on weekdays, looked up as she stepped in and said, "Ah, there you are. It's about time!"

Ashley glanced at her watch. "I'm not late," she said mildly.

"Aren't you? Maybe it just felt like it, then. It's been a long week."

"Has it? Why's that?"

Jack sighed. "The Great McGraw. He's driving me crazy."

That didn't surprise Ashley one bit. She knew the feeling. "I gather he's not here," she said, relieved and disappointed at the same time.

Jack looked surprised. "No, why should he be?"

"I don't know, I just thought——"

"As a matter of fact, you can thank your stars he isn't," Jack interrupted. "I've seen more than enough of him this week. Always barging in when he's not wanted, full of ideas about displays and promotions, and things he says I ought to be doing. Oh, and Dan from Kenora phoned. McGraw's been giving him the gears too. Bloody new broom! He's even ordered one of those fancy new cash registers. The customers will love it," he finished gloomily.

Ashley hid a smile. Jack had always taken a very dim view of "the public" who were the reason for his having a job. Any innovation that found favor with a customer was unlikely to win Brownie points with Jack.

"What's more," he was going on, "McGraw says I have to be more enthusiastic, and work harder. What does he know?"

"I know that as your boss I expect maximum effort and a minimum of excuses for slacking off," said a hard voice from the doorway.

Ashley jumped as wind and snow swirled across the threshold and the door slammed shut behind her.

Jack, who had also had his back to the entrance, gulped noisily, and she found herself reluctantly applauding Gray for attempting to light a fire under his lethargic employee. Mr. Boyko, intent on selling the business, hadn't cared much as long as no one complained.

"I—er—um," stuttered Jack, "I didn't mean..."

"Yes, you did. And I meant what I said too. If you want to keep your job you'll damn well shape up and do something about your attitude. I'm used to captaining a team that gives me everything it's got, and I don't accept stalling or excuses. Got that?" Gray shook the snow from his jacket and flung it over the counter.

Jack nodded, muttered, "Yes—sir," and sidled off to the back to fetch his coat. A minute later, after a mumbled good-night, he scuttled through the door like a chastened child.

Ashley eyed Gray doubtfully, wondering if his ill-humor was about to descend on her. While she had to agree that Jack had had it coming to him, she couldn't help feeling that it wouldn't have hurt Gray to be a little less autocratic—especially in front of another employee.

She said so. "You could have been more diplomatic," she reproached him.

"I haven't time for diplomacy. He got the message."

"Oh, yes, he got the message all right. Is that why you came in? To ruin his weekend?"

"Judging from my observation of that young man, he deserves to have it ruined. But no, that is *not* why I came in. I have to be somewhere in a short while, and, as it hardly seemed worth going home for half an hour, I decided to drop in on my property."

She heard the small emphasis on the "my" and knew she had just been rebuked. Gray didn't like his actions to be questioned, as she had good reason to know.

"Oh," she said, ignoring his censure, and hoping he didn't think his "property" included her.

He eyed her with an expression she suspected was intended to challenge, and said equably, "I expected you to phone me, Ashley."

"Phone you? Why would I do that?" What was he talking about now?

"I thought for sure you'd ring up to accuse me of sexual harassment, and refuse to work for me any longer."

"I would have, if I'd thought of it," said Ashley.

Gray brushed a hand quickly over his lips. "That's my girl," he said approvingly. "I didn't think you'd let me down." When she opened her mouth to reply, he added, "You have the most splendidly indignant-looking back, you know. Especially when you've just been hit on the nose by a snowflake. I was sure I'd have to start interviewing new help."

Ashley glowered. "You couldn't possibly have seen the snowflake," she retorted.

"I have an excellent imagination." His eyes wandered contemplatively over her bulky parka and came to rest somewhere below her thighs.

Blast him and his imagination, thought Ashley. But aloud she only said coolly, "I see. Well, since I haven't quit, and you haven't fired me——"

"Yet."

"Yet—if you don't mind, I'd like to take my coat off before any customers arrive."

He nodded. "That's what I like to see. Dutiful dedication to my interests."

Ashley lifted her chin and started to peel off her parka, at which point he nodded again and said, "Besides, I much prefer the uncensored view." His voice was dry, but he made no attempt at all to disguise his appreciation of her neat pink sweater and nicely fitting navy blue pants.

"If you just came in to annoy me..." began Ashley through barely parted lips.

"I didn't. I came in to kiss you."

She pulled herself up to her full, not very impressive height. "Mr. McGraw, you are my employer. I think you should remember that."

"Oh, I hadn't forgotten," he assured her, with that twisted smile that always liquefied her knees. He glanced at his watch and his expression changed. "On second thoughts, as it seems I haven't time to do the job properly after all, perhaps we'll put it off until tomorrow."

Ashley drew in her breath and prepared to deliver a blistering retort. Then she realized it would be totally wasted, because Gray was already heading for the door, and the look on his face when he turned to lift his hand

in farewell was no longer casually teasing and pro-
voking. It was troubled—and surprisingly urgent.

She frowned as the door swung shut behind him. What
on earth was that all about? Really, he was the most
infuriating man. Every time she met him, she felt a
stronger and stronger urge to slap his face. Unfortunately, she also felt an irritating desire to kiss him.

Her frown deepened. Why the sudden urgency? One
minute he was making lazily suggestive remarks, the next
he was hurrying away as if he was late for an important
engagement. With whom, then? Ashley tightened her
lips. It wasn't her concern, and she'd do well to remember that.

All the same, as she replenished shelves, swept a pile
of dust from the floor, and performed all the duties Jack
had neglected, she couldn't help wondering if Gray's
sudden haste had something to do with a woman...

She dropped two boxes of skates onto the floor, swore
silently, and bent down to pick them up.

The evening passed fairly quietly after that, but, to
her surprise, Ashley found herself getting restless. She
sighed. There was no getting away from it, Gray's demanding presence certainly added spice to the routine.
With him around, she might go home mad, but at least
she couldn't complain that she was bored.

By halfway through the following day, she would have
traded spice and a week's wages for boredom. There was
an unending stream of customers, all clamoring, and
most of them wanting items Jack hadn't ordered. On
top of that, two mothers came in with crying babies,
and three special deliveries didn't turn up—one of them,
inevitably, intended for Mrs. Cartwright. Ashley had just
picked up a baseball bat, and was contemplating a spot
of assault and battery on two teenage boys who were
engaged in a feud to the death on the floor, when Gray
walked in.

He took one look at Ashley's face, seized the two boys by the scruffs of their necks and ejected them ungently. Then, after throwing off his jacket and rolling up his sleeves, he set to work to restore order. In no time at all, following a couple of crisp phone calls, the missing deliveries had arrived, the items Jack hadn't ordered were on the way and, to Ashley's amazement, Gray, with a slightly fixed smile on his face, was waiting efficiently on a line of awed customers. Somewhat to her chagrin, he was very good at it. He teased the children, who took to him at once, and talked intelligently to the adults, even when he had to admit he didn't know much about the items they were buying.

When the last customer finally left, he pulled out a handkerchief, ran it around the back of his neck, and remarked, "That was quite an afternoon, wasn't it? And I thought *hockey* was a contact sport."

Ashley smiled, a little warily. "Yes, I'm sorry. It's not always as chaotic as that. Usually I can cope."

"I'm sure you can. On the other hand, I defy anyone under a hundred and eighty pounds to cope with Mrs. Cartwright. You should have seen her and that young beanpole going at it hammer and tongs over our last goalie stick! We'll have to order some more, by the way."

"Who won?" asked Ashley.

"I did. Mrs. Cartwright broke the stick, and I made her pay for it."

Ashley choked. "Good for you! Mrs. Cartwright and her kids are always breaking things, but Mr. Boyko never managed to get a dime back out of them."

"I have my methods," said Gray, balancing himself on the corner of the counter and smiling cynically. "Does that mean I've gone up in your estimation, or does it make me more of a bastard?"

She stared at the long legs extended straight in front of him, at the muscular arms crossed on the black-shirted chest, and then she let her gaze travel on up to his face. His dark hair had fallen untidily across his forehead, he was still smiling, and his eyes were filled with devilish silver lights. Oh, yes, he was certainly a bastard. But he'd never been all that down in her estimation. He was too damned attractive.

"Both, I expect," she said ruefully. "I'm glad you made Mrs. Cartwright pay, but I think you did it by being unscrupulous."

"Not at all. I merely told her that the last time a kid came into my shop and deliberately broke something I'd tanned his backside for him."

Ashley gasped. "You didn't!"

"Didn't what? Tan Mrs. Cartwright's backside?" He shuddered. "Quite right, I didn't."

She giggled. "Idiot. I mean you didn't really hit a kid, did you?"

"No, but she didn't know that."

Ashley shook her head. "I knew you'd been unscrupulous."

He sighed. "I can't win with you, can I? And, that being the case, suppose I drive you home now? Even I have the odd chivalrous instinct, and it's cold out there."

"No, thanks," she said quickly.

His eyes narrowed. "Why not? Afraid you'll kiss me again? Or afraid I won't?"

"Neither," snapped Ashley. "I just don't need a ride."

Gray shook his head. "Don't cut off your pretty nose to spite your face. I'll behave myself—if you insist."

His smile was so seductive that her heart turned over, and although she still didn't trust him an inch suddenly his offer was irresistible. Besides, it *was* cold out there.

"All right." She smiled back sheepishly. "Thank you. A ride would be nice."

Gray was the soul of decorum on the way to her house, and the only awkward moment came when she ventured to ask what had brought him into the shop.

"You did," he replied tersely, in a tone that left her wondering what she'd done. When he didn't even offer to fasten her seat belt, Ashley didn't know whether she was pleased or sorry.

The one thing she did know, when she stood on the pavement beside him as he helped her out of the car, was that she wished her mother wasn't sailing down the path with her arms outstretched and a welcoming smile splitting her broad face.

"Come in, come in," cried Rosa. "Join us for supper, why don't you? There's plenty for all of us—the more the merrier."

Ashley groaned under her breath. "No, Mom, I'm sure Gray has plans," she began desperately.

"No, he hasn't," murmured a low voice in her ear.

"And I don't think..." She stopped. What didn't she think? Well, for a start, she didn't think she could stand the idea of Gray, who had never had to put up with brothers and sisters, raising his fascinating dark eyebrows at the antics of her obstreperous family. They annoyed her a lot of the time too, but they *were* her family, and she didn't take kindly to criticism from outside sources. Nor could she tolerate the thought of Maria and Sophia making embarrassingly speculative remarks about Gray's relationship with their sister.

"It's not a good idea, Mom," she said loudly, as Rosa bustled up to them.

"It's a wonderful idea," Gray contradicted her, turning his crooked smile on Ashley's well-upholstered mother. "Thank you, Mrs. Kalani." He hesitated, then added in a curiously flat voice, "But I hope you won't mind my leaving early."

"Of course not," said Rosa who, unlike Ashley, did read the sports pages and knew all about Gray's living arrangements. "You'll want to get home to your father. Poor man, all those years with no one to do his cooking for him..."

Gray shook his head. "He could have had all the cooks he wanted. He preferred to look after himself."

Ashley wondered why his voice still sounded flat. She also wondered what on earth made her mother think that a man like Gray would be in a hurry to get home to his *father*. Then she stopped caring, because Rosa, beaming from ear to ear, had taken his arm and was towing him up the path to the front door.

She muttered something under her breath that she knew her mother would take exception to, and followed glumly in their wake.

"Did you say something, Ashley?" asked Gray over his shoulder.

She could only see one of his eyes, but it held the sort of glitter that she knew was intended to rile her.

"No," she said grimly, "I didn't."

He lifted his shoulder. "Funny, I could have sworn you did."

Ashley didn't answer.

As soon as the door closed behind them their eardrums were assaulted by the inevitable sound of a Kalani family dispute. Ashley groaned again. She might have known.

"Mom!" It was Nick's boyish treble this time, screaming from the top of the stairs. "Mom, Rocky's in the bath with his boots on. And he's locked the door!"

Of course he's locked the door, thought Ashley. How else could you get privacy in this house?

"With his boots on!" exclaimed Rosa, raising her voice to shout at the guilty occupant of the bathtub. "Rocky, what's this your brother's telling me?"

An unintelligible mumble drifted down the stairs in reply, and Nick said quickly, "He's soaking them."

"Why, in heaven's name? His new boots?"

"He says he's trying to make them fit his feet."

"Fit his feet! They did fit his feet. I'll give him fit . . ."

Rosa heaved her bulk up the stairs, leaving Gray and Ashley standing in the hallway. Nick, smiling smugly, slithered around his mother and came to join them.

"You'd better come into the living room, Gray," said Ashley hopelessly. "There's only my dad in there. He's playing Wagner."

Now why had she said that? Only the profoundly deaf could be unaware that Toivo was playing Wagner. As they approached the living room the walls were shaking.

"Nick," she said, turning to her brother, "why did you have to tell Mom about Rocky's boots?"

"'Cos he's not s'posed to," replied Nick, looking virtuous.

Gray glanced down at him and smiled grimly. "As the damage was already done, what you really mean, young man, is that you couldn't miss the chance to stir up trouble. Isn't that right?"

Nick squirmed and hung his head.

"Of course it is," said Ashley bitterly. "No one around here ever misses a chance to stir up trouble."

"Now, now, Ashley!" Toivo, taking them all by surprise, had turned down the stereo as they came in, just in time to hear his daughter's comment. "You know that's not true."

"No, Dad," she agreed tiredly, "of course it isn't." It *was*, more or less, but she didn't want to argue in front of Gray who, exactly as she had predicted, was raising a superior eyebrow at her and looking amused.

"This is my father," she introduced him quickly. "Dad, this is Gray McGraw."

"And I'm Nick," said Nick, "and I didn't mean to make trouble, Mr. McGraw. Mom doesn't really mean it when she yells."

"Nick's a fan of yours," explained Ashley. Although she didn't approve of her young brother telling tales, she knew he'd be heartbroken if he thought he'd earned his idol's disapproval.

Gray understood.

"I'm sure she doesn't," he agreed, putting a friendly hand on Nick's anxious auburn head. At once the boy's eyes widened worshipfully.

Toivo stood up. "Have a seat, Gray McGraw. It's an honor to meet you."

I can't stand, it, thought Ashley.

"I'll leave Dad and Nick to entertain you," she mumbled at Gray, her eyes slanting away from his smile. "I'll see if Mom needs help in the kitchen . . ."

But when she reached the kitchen, Rosa, fresh from her confrontation about boots, immediately tried to shoo her away.

"Out," she said firmly. "You go and look after your young man. You ought to cultivate that one. He's single, with time on his hands, and he's rich. He'll want to settle down. You ought to be nice to him, Ashley." She nodded, agreeing with her own pronouncements. "Yes, indeed. He's nice-looking too."

"Mom! He's not my young man, and I don't want a husband. I want to get my degree and look after myself. Besides, I don't even like him."

"Nonsense," said Rosa. "He likes you."

"No, he doesn't. He just likes baiting me."

"That's what I mean. He likes you."

Ashley gave up and began to pull plates out of the cupboard.

Supper in the long family dining room was just as disastrous as she had feared. Gray's eyes opened very wide when they fell on the garish sunsets and purple mountains selected by Rosa to "brighten up" the pale cream walls. Sophia and Maria giggled and made sly remarks, Gina grumbled intermittently about broccoli, cucumbers, eggs and anything else that wasn't dessert, and Rocky and Carlo carried on a loud argument about the relative merits of two local rock bands, both of which Ashley considered awful. Nick and Toivo, ignoring the rest of the family, shouted rapid-fire questions at Gray about his past career.

Ashley sat stoically swallowing food which she couldn't taste, determined to get through this meal without exploding. She wasn't in the habit of exploding and she would have made it without difficulty this time—if only, in the midst of all the babble, Gray hadn't turned away from Nick to rake his eyes over her very slowly and ask with a deceptively innocent smile, "Lost your voice, Ashley? I've never known you at a loss for words before." When she continued to crunch cucumber in glowering silence, he added pensively, "It makes a change. Quite an improvement, in fact."

"But Ashley's always quiet," said Sophia, looking startled.

"Is she? You could have fooled me." The words were directed at Sophia, but the white-toothed grin that accompanied them was aimed quite devastatingly at Ashley. It wasn't a particularly warm grin either. It put her in mind of a wolf about to pounce.

"I didn't think anyone could fool you," she said sourly. "You always seem to have all the answers."

To her surprise, as the chatter resumed all around them after a moment's embarrassed quiet, the wolfish look disappeared. It was almost as if a shutter had closed over his face.

"Not all the answers," he said brusquely, giving her a small, hard smile.

Ashley, who hadn't wanted him to be here in the first place, felt as if she'd just been slapped in the face. It wasn't what he'd said. It was how he'd said it. And suddenly she couldn't stay in the room a moment longer. "Excuse me," she muttered, jumping to her feet and hurrying out to the kitchen.

She scraped the remains of her meal into the garbage and leaned against the counter with her eyes closed. After a while Rosa came in. For once, after a quick look at Ashley's face, she only said, "Take your father and Gray their coffee, will you, dear?"

Ashley nodded dumbly.

"Well? Did you enjoy that?" she challenged Gray, when she carried the coffee into the living room and slapped a cup down beside him.

"Very much," he replied. "Are you disappointed?"

Once again, Ashley was too stunned and angry to answer.

She had no difficulty finding her voice, though, when, only a few minutes later, he insisted that she accompany him to the gate.

"I'm sorry I have to leave early," he said abruptly.

"I'm not. And you had no business accepting Mom's invitation," she told him crossly. "You knew I didn't want you to stay."

"Listen, young lady," he said, catching her arm and swinging her around to face him, "I'm getting a bit tired of constantly being told I'm in the way. What is it with you? Is my company so repulsive?"

"Sometimes it is," said Ashley, staring hard at the frozen ground. "But it's not that."

"What is it, then?" She could feel his leather-gloved fingers tightening through the heavy folds of her coat.

"It's just that—my family—they're so—so noisy, so—oh, I don't know. And you were nice to them, and horrible to me at supper. I knew you'd hate it."

"I didn't hate it. I liked your family. And you, my girl, need a good swift kick in the right place to wake you up. Remind me to administer it some time. Don't you realize how damn lucky you are to have a family like that? Sure they're noisy, and they bicker a lot—families do. But you all care about each other, don't you? That's what counts."

"Yes, of course we do. It's just that I thought you——"

"You thought I was too good for them, I suppose—or thought I thought I was." He put both hands on her shoulders and gave her a brisk shake. "You ought to be ashamed of yourself, Ashley. And for heaven's sake give me *some* credit for recognizing good, decent people when I meet them."

"I'm sorry," she said stiffly, turning her face away to stare bleakly back at the house. "Funny, I thought *I'd* be the one defending my family to you. Not the other way around."

There was an odd little break in her voice, and Gray said more gently, "You don't have to defend them, Ashley. They're great people. I only wish——" He stopped. "Never mind. I have to get moving. Good night."

His voice was so curt that Ashley looked up, startled, her lips parting a little in surprise. And to her even greater surprise, he bent down and brushed his mouth across them. It was cold, but firm somehow. Nice. She wished he would do it again.

But he didn't. He only touched her lightly on the cheek with one leather-clad finger, and swung himself into his car.

Ashley, her emotions churning about like swirling snow, walked slowly back to the house. She wondered where he'd gone in such a hurry...

Over the next couple of days, with exams looming, she tried to put Gray out of her mind. But it didn't work. She couldn't forget the way he could be so hard and full of mockery one moment, so amusing and helpful the next. And on top of that, her mind kept returning, again and again, to that embarrassing conversation by the gate.

Because he was right. There was no doubt of that. She *did* have a great family, and she shouldn't have been ashamed to let Gray meet them. He'd proved without question that he was big enough to see past the bickering and shouting, to the warmth and affection underneath. He'd even seemed to like all the racket and commotion.

Ashley frowned, and stabbed her pencil hard into the pad on which she was meant to be taking notes. It was odd that Gray had been so angry with her, almost as if he wanted to punish her for not appreciating something *he'd* never had. She thought about that. Come to think of it, of course, he couldn't have had a normal family life. Not with his mother dead, and a childhood constantly preoccupied with sport. As well, there was something strange about the way he reacted whenever his father came up in the conversation. Yes, it *was* odd...

Her pencil snapped, and she groped in her bag for another. The lecturer was droning on about Canadian economics, but her mind wouldn't stay on the dreary topic, because—she had to face it—Gray had made her feel like a little girl again—one who didn't know how to behave. And that made her angry. Even if he was right. It also made her feel guilty. Then she wondered irritably why it mattered. Why should she care what Gray thought? He was her boss, that was all, and, as long as she performed the job to his satisfaction, what he thought about her personally didn't count.

She fixed her gaze firmly on the lecturer's bearded face and vowed not to think of Gray again. At least not until the weekend—when of course there was no reason whatever to imagine he might visit the shop...

When she arrived at work on Friday, Jack was standing behind the counter with a face that resembled green cheese.

"He's put me on probation," he told Ashley. "Says if I don't shape up he'll have to let me go."

"Don't worry, we're both on probation," said Ashley, who thought privately that Gray was on the right track with regard to Jack.

"You're not. He's been in every day this week, checking up. And he keeps talking about you, holding you up as an example. Says you'd have made a good hockey player. Aggressive, committed, willing to work your a——"

"I'm not aggressive," Ashley interrupted hotly. "He's no right to say that!"

"He doesn't need rights. He makes his own."

Ashley had occasion to remember Jack's words when she arrived on the job the following day to find Gray in the storeroom turning the air blue because he couldn't find any coffee.

"It's in that drawer," she said, pointing.

"Hmm. Make some, then."

"What did you say?"

"I said make some coffee, for goodness' sake!"

Obviously he'd gotten out on the wrong side of the bed this morning, but she didn't see why that meant she had to take it.

"I'll show you how to make it, if you like," she said sweetly.

"Like hell you will! Why do you think I hired you?"

"To help in the shop, among other things."

"Right. And 'other things' means coffee."

Ashley glared at him. He was dressed all in black again, and with his fists pressed into the small table he was glowering at her over the top of the coffeemaker looking like some dangerous and very large animal intent on devouring everything in its path. In this case, everything happened to be her.

The truth of the matter was that she didn't in the least mind making coffee. She had often done it for Mr. Boyko when he came in. But she did mind being treated as a lowly slave by the great hockey hero, who was apparently used to being waited on hand and foot—and who was also, for some reason, in an exceptionally foul mood this morning.

"Afraid you won't be able to figure it out?" she taunted him. "It's not hard. You just fill the pot with water——"

Gray's eyebrows lowered in an ugly scowl, and for a moment she thought he was going to hit her. But in the end, after an agonizingly tense moment in which two pairs of dark eyes locked in what could have turned into mortal combat, he slammed his fist on the table, shaking several packages of sugar onto the floor, growled a few choice words that Ashley didn't think she'd heard before, and strode off out of the room.

She leaned back against the wall, feeling limp.

That Gray was in a very bad temper required no spelling out. But what in the world was behind that ridiculous scene? Had he had a fight with his father? It didn't seem likely. He was too old for childish rebellions. With a woman, then? Ashley paused in the act of reaching for the coffee, surprised to feel a quick flare of—oh, no! Oh, no. *Not* jealousy. *Please* not jealousy, she prayed, raising her eyes to the ceiling.

"Of course not jealousy," she answered herself out loud. "What nonsense!" Snapping a filter open, she filled it with coffee and marched off to fetch the water.

It was against her principles to give in to Gray, but he seemed to be in need of coffee. It might improve his temper. And she'd made her point.

When she handed the steaming mug to him, he was hunched over the cash register glaring at two customers who were getting out of their car.

"You'll scare them away if you keep that up," she told him. "Why don't you go drink this in the back?"

"Hm." His eyes flicked over her as he took the mug from her, his jaw still jutting aggressively. Then without a word he turned his back and stalked down the aisle to the storeroom.

Why can't the back of him in a temper look just plain silly—like my brothers? thought Ashley as she watched him go. Why does he have to be so damn sexy?

There wasn't any answer to that, and there were customers coming in, so she put on her best smile and went to help them.

About half an hour later, when the store began to fill up with Christmas shoppers, Gray reappeared.

"Can you cope?" he asked shortly.

"Of course."

He nodded and swung off through the door carrying the inventory book she supposed he had come to collect.

At ten to five, when the store finally emptied, he reappeared and, ignoring her completely, strode to the back of the shop. Then, just as she was putting the cover on the new cash register, he came back carrying a mug of coffee which he dumped down beside her on the counter. It smelled strong, spicy and enticing.

"With my compliments," he growled. "I should have known you'd make a lousy slave."

"Is that supposed to be an apology?" exclaimed Ashley, putting her hands on her hips and wondering whether she ought to laugh or slap him.

"If you like. It's all you're going to get, I'm afraid. I'm not much good at apologies."

She noted the stubborn set to his mouth, but for a fleeting instant she had an impression that the gleam in his eye might be of the sheepish variety. As apologies went, she supposed this was the best she could hope for.

"All right," she said, shrugging her shoulders, "I suppose I'll have to forgive you—this time."

"Thank you. Madam." His slanting smile was not nearly as repentant as it might have been, but, to her chagrin, she found herself smiling back.

"I'll drive you home," he said authoritatively. "Fetch your coat."

"Oh, no," said Ashley. "No way." She swallowed. "What you said—about my family. You were right, of course. But you're not——"

"I'm not getting myself invited to supper again? Quite true—I'm not. I have other plans, as it happens."

"Oh," said Ashley, feeling foolish, and wondering if his other plans involved the woman he'd had a fight with.

"Yes—oh. Now fetch your coat."

Ashley fetched it.

"Wait," he said, as she started to pull it on.

She blinked. "What for?"

"There's something I have to find out." Without explaining, he took the coat and flung it across the counter.

"What do you think you're doing...?" she began.

"This."

As she gaped at him, he put his hands on her shoulders and drew her toward him. She was still gaping when he lowered his lips over hers, and with practiced efficiency began to probe the warm sweet depths of her mouth.

"Mmph," she murmured, trying to pull away, and stunned by an overwhelming longing to respond. More than anything now she wanted to return his kiss. But she wasn't going to. Returning it could easily prove fatal.

After an endless time, during which spears of fire seemed to pierce every nerve end in her body, Gray lifted his head and smiled down at her. He looked quite calm and unshaken.

"Mmm, very satisfactory," he murmured. "And you do."

"Do what?" gulped Ashley.

"Taste just as nice as I remembered."

"Oh! Of all the—— Gray McGraw, you're supposed to be my boss. I—I *will* charge you with harassment . . ."

"Will you indeed? Then we'd better make sure the charge sticks, hadn't we?"

"What do you——?" Her words were cut off as Gray's hands moved from her shoulders to her waist, then dropped down to spread out over her bottom.

As Ashley bit back a cry that was half delicious excitement, half indignation, he pulled her up hard against his body, so that she could feel every muscle in his chest— and, when his fingers began to stroke lightly over the tight fabric of her pants, she felt something else, and knew a wild moment of exultation that the cool indifference he had assumed was just a facade.

Then her control broke, and she couldn't remain stiff and unresponsive any more. The cry she had been holding in sounded softly in her ears as she wound her arms around his neck and pulled his face down to hers.

She felt him tense for a second, then he was kissing her with a dark, hungry passion that sent her senses reeling with delight. All caution gone, she returned his kiss without inhibition, and knew for the second time the sweet, unbelievable warmth of her own desire.

They stayed like that for a long time, but Gray was the one who finally raised his head and, still with his arms around her, looked down into her eyes and said softly, "Well? Do you feel suitably harassed?"

Ashley turned her head away. *"Why?"* she whispered. "Why, Gray?"

"The same reason as last time. I wanted to."

She nodded dumbly, feeling a disconcerting moisture in her eyes. "I see. Yes, I—I seem to remember hearing once that you play the mating game the same way you play hockey. That when you want a woman you just wade right in and collect her—using force if you have to. I guess it's true."

"Not necessarily." His black, brooding gaze seemed to be boring a hole in her cheekbone, so she looked away. "I told you, I haven't had much time for serious romance. And I'm not interested in collecting any woman unless she's willing to be collected."

"And you think I am?"

He put his fingers beneath her chin and made her look at him. "Mmm. Yes, I do. Do you still plan to charge me with harassment?" His mouth slanted in a quizzical curl.

Ashley shook her head. "No. It wouldn't be true."

"Spoken like an honest woman! Which I think you are. Now tell me something else."

"What?"

"If I asked you to go to bed with me, what would you say?"

Ashley gasped. "I'd say no," she replied immediately, not giving herself time to think.

"I see." He dropped his hand and it brushed, featherlike, against her breast before coming to rest against his thigh.

"It's not that I don't—like you," said Ashley, wondering why she was bothering to explain. "It's just something I don't do, that's all. Besides, just like you, I haven't the time."

"Hmm, I suppose I asked for that."

"Yes," said Ashley, taking a deep breath. "And Gray, this isn't going to work."

"What isn't?"

"My working here."

"Ah. You mean I'm so irresistible that sooner or later I'll manage to wear you down?"

She saw that he was grinning in that mocking way that so particularly annoyed her—even as it continued to charm her.

"Certainly not. Well, something like that," she admitted, not wanting to lie, and yet unwilling to admit that he'd just about hit the nail on the head.

"In that case I think you'd better stay," he said, the grin becoming positively outrageous.

"I can't. I'm sorry, Gray, you'll have to get someone else."

"Don't be a fool! You said yourself you needed the job. And I can use your help. The fact that I could also do with your body has nothing to do with it——"

"It has *everything* to do with it," cried Ashley.

"Oh, for heaven's sake!" He was glaring at her now, once more looking like some restless animal on the prowl. "These aren't the Dark Ages, Ashley. I'm not going to force myself on you. Nor would the world come to an end if I happened to take you to bed."

"Mine would," said Ashley simply.

Gray rolled his eyes up. "'Give me chastity and self-restraint,'" he muttered, "'but do not give it yet.'"

Ashley blinked. "What?"

"St. Augustine. He must have seen you coming."

"More likely he saw *you* coming," she retorted, frowning. Imagine Gray quoting St. Augustine at her. Would he never cease to amaze her?

After what was obviously a considerable struggle to hold his temper in check, Gray shook his head. "Okay," he growled, "you win. I need you, Ashley. In the *store*," he added, as he saw her mouth open to protest. "I have other matters on my mind at the moment, personal ones, and I need competent help here with Christmas coming. Young Jack's not pulling his weight. So stay." His jaw tightened, and he finished with an obvious effort, *"Please."*

Ashley pulled at the neck of her sweater. "I don't know..."

She saw the flare of exasperation in his eyes. "I said you win. I promise not to lay a finger on you. And I won't even mention that I own a bed. I'll be the boss, you'll be the staff, and our relationship will be entirely..." He hesitated. "I was going to say platonic, but I don't suppose that's possible."

"Try moral," suggested Ashley.

"Huh! Puritanical, you mean. It makes no sense, to my mind, but, if that's the way you want it, that's the way it will have to be."

His voice was rough, his mouth pulled into a flat line. But Ashley knew that he meant it. He was exasperated—frustrated too, probably—but he would keep his promise.

"I'll think about it," she said quietly. "I'll let you know on Monday, if that's all right."

"It's not all right, but I suppose it will have to be, won't it? Come on, then, I said I'd drive you home."

"You don't have to."

"I *know* I don't have to. I said I'm going to. So let's get moving, I've got a lot to do this evening."

Ashley considered pointing out that he was the one who had held them up, but he looked so large and male and domineering standing there ordering her to move that she decided it would be wiser to hold her peace.

Gray drove her home very fast and in complete silence, but it wasn't a silence she had much interest in breaking. She was far too busy with her own chaotic emotions.

When he dropped her off, he said, "Good night, Ashley," very formally, and didn't even try to take her hand.

On Monday evening Jack phoned almost as soon as she got in the door.

He told her that Gray had just fired him. Without notice.

CHAPTER FIVE

"WHAT?" cried Ashley. "But he can't do that."

"He has," Jack said bitterly.

"But it's illegal."

"No. He's given me two months' pay in lieu of notice."

"Oh, Jack, I *am* sorry. What are you going to do?"

"I'm going to work at the supermarket across the road. For more money."

"Well, but that's great——"

"No, it's not. The manager over there's a slave driver. Always on your back about something, the guys tell me. I *liked* working for old Boyko."

Yes, thought Ashley. Old Boyko, who hadn't noticed or cared much that his employee was letting him down.

"Still, you were lucky to get the supermarket job so quickly," she pointed out, deciding to accentuate the positive.

"Yeah, I guess so." Jack didn't sound convinced. "See you around, Ash. Just thought I'd let you know. Good luck with the fiend."

"Fiend?"

"McGraw. He was in a foul temper all day."

"What else is new?" scoffed Ashley. "Bye, Jack. Good luck." She hung up the phone with a sigh and trailed upstairs to sink down on the edge of her bed.

So Gray had actually done it. She frowned, realizing that his abrupt dismissal of Jack left her with more doubts about him than ever.

She stared at the picture of Great-Aunt Dorinda, which sat on her bedside table because no one else in the house would give it space.

It wasn't so much that Gray had let Jack go that disturbed her. It was the way he had done it. Sure, he'd warned Jack, but it *was* just before Christmas, and he could have waited, given the young man another chance. After all, it was no thanks to Gray that Jack had found another job so quickly. She shook her head unhappily. Firing the lackadaisical Jack so soon after he had taken over the shop smacked of a certain ruthlessness in Gray that she didn't like, and couldn't easily accept. But she supposed he'd always been ruthless and a little brutal. He'd had to be, to survive in his chosen field.

Which brought her to the crucial decision.

Should she stay on to work for Gray, or follow her instincts and get out while the going was good? Before she found herself embroiled in something she had always succeeded in avoiding, with a man who fascinated and attracted her as no man had ever done before? A man who was arrogant and overbearing, and who could, and almost certainly would, hurt her. Apart from which, she didn't in the least trust him. He made no bones about wanting to make love to her, but he kept dashing off on urgent and mysterious appointments. And it didn't take much imagination to figure out the probable nature of those appointments. Not with a man as physical as Gray...

She glared at Great-Aunt Dorinda, who glared right back. *That* was why she was so sure Gray would hurt her. He wanted an affair, pure and simple, now that he had time to indulge in what he called "serious romance"—and by which he probably meant serious lust. She, on the other hand, had never wanted that. If, some time in the future, she found she was ready for commitment, then she knew she would want it to be forever.

But right now, as she had told him quite truthfully, she just hadn't the time. Even if she had, Gray, with his moods and short temper, his abrupt departures, his arrogant expectation that if he wanted something he would get it—and yes, even his gift of easy laughter—was not the right man for her. Besides, if he already had a woman in tow, she was damned if she was going to become just another item in his collection.

She stood up, and, calling to her mother that she had to go out again, made her way purposefully down the stairs. She had spent all day yesterday, and half of today, trying to decide if she could work with Gray and still maintain a sensibly platonic distance. Now she had her answer.

"You're still here," said Ashley, half an hour later, after taking the bus to head office and finding that, although most of the staff had gone home, the big front door of the substantial brick building was still open. Gray, in his shirtsleeves, was in his office staring down at a computer printout.

"Well, I'm not a bloody ghost. Of course I'm here," he snapped.

Belatedly, she wondered why she hadn't thought to phone, instead of bearding the lion in his lair.

He went on studying the printout on his desk, and she glanced quickly around the office. In Mr. Boyko's day it had contained two smallish metal tables, a comfortable chair and a couple of tatty rugs covering a scratched wood floor. Now it sported a thick gold carpet, one large mahogany desk, and a high-backed black executive chair. Several very good sporting prints hung on the walls, which had been painted a rich cream color. Ashley wrinkled her nose. Either Gray liked elegant surroundings for their own sake, or else he had the good sense to know that a prosperous image often bred further prosperity.

She watched as he ran his thumb down to the bottom of the page in front of him, then glanced up. "What can I do for you?" he asked, quite pleasantly now.

Ashley straightened her shoulders. "You fired Jack," she said accusingly.

"I'm aware of that." His eyes returned to the printout.

She tightened her lips. "You could have given him another chance, couldn't you?"

"He's had dozens of chances. And don't tell me how to run my business."

Hmm, thought Ashley. Obviously Jack had got it right. Gray was in a fiendish mood today. Well, that was tough, because she was about to make it worse, and she didn't care.

"All right," she said to his bent head, "I won't. You can run your business any way you like, because I won't be working for you any more." He raised his eyes again at that, and she saw that they were cool and uncompromising.

"I'm sorry," she said stiffly.

"Why, Ashley?" he asked. "Because I fired Jack? Or because I'd like to take you to bed?"

"Both," she said, annoyed by his brusqueness, and surprisingly hurt by his seeming lack of concern.

He punched both fists onto his desk and bent toward her across the wide expanse of mahogany. "In other words, you don't trust me."

No, she didn't trust him. How could she, when he kept so much of himself hidden? But she didn't entirely trust herself either. "No, I don't altogether——" she began doubtfully.

"For heaven's sake, Ashley! Can't you understand...?" He paused, then started again in a more neutral tone. "Is it really necessary to desert me now? Just before Christmas, when I already have Jack to replace?"

"That's your fault, isn't it?"

He didn't answer, but his eyes, when they came to rest on her, glinted with a speculative light. It was almost as if he were contemplating a particularly intransigent child, and wondering if he should deal with her in time-honored fashion. It would be just like him, she thought grimly, but if he tried it he'd get more than he bargained for.

Apparently he decided against it.

"Ashley, there's no reason for you to leave," he said crisply. "I made you a promise."

"I know you did, and I expect you meant it. I just don't think it's a good idea. But if you need help in the shop, you can have Maria. This is her last year at school and she's looking for a part-time job. She's worked at Boyko's before, so she knows what she's doing."

"I don't want Maria. I want you."

And how! thought Ashley. "You can't have me," she replied calmly, "so Maria will just have to do. Provided you behave yourself, McGraw."

"Behave my—— For heaven's sake, Ashley, what do you take me for? Maria's only a kid. And I just told you, I don't——"

"I know. You don't want her, you want me. But I'm not coming back, Gray."

She saw his chest expand under the white shirt as he took a long, deep breath. "You *are* afraid of me." He gave a short, hard laugh. "Well, you're not the first one, but from you I don't find it flattering. All right, if you won't reconsider——"

"No," said Ashley, who didn't have a reputation for knowing her own mind for nothing. "I'm sorry, Gray, but I won't. And I'm not afraid of you." When he didn't reply, she added brightly, "So—would you like me to send you Maria?"

"Not particularly. How is she at handling Mrs. Cartwright?"

Ashley tried to suppress a smile. "Not as good as you."

He caught the lighter note in her voice and pounced on it. "Ashley, don't be so damned obstinate! Do as you're told for once, and stay."

"No."

Quietly and with great precision, Gray displayed further evidence of his grasp of some of the more esoteric variations on the English language. This was followed by an abrupt silence.

"Do I have a choice? About Maria?" he asked finally.

"Of course. You're free to hire whomever you choose."

"Except you."

"Right. Except me."

His jaw hardened, and his broad shoulders shrugged at his shirt.

"Okay," he said, so harshly that she jumped and hit her hand on the desk. "Okay, send Maria. And don't worry, I won't eat her."

"I didn't think you would," said Ashley, not quite truthfully.

He stared at her, then gestured at the door. "Well? What are you waiting for?"

"Nothing, I...nothing." She spun on her heel and hurried toward the exit, well aware that she was reacting to him like a frightened mouse—which was probably exactly what he intended. But if she didn't get out quickly she knew she would be unable to restrain an almost overpowering impulse to pick up his large brass paperweight and hurl it at his arrogant head. What's more, she thought viciously, I wouldn't miss!

But just as she reached the door she could have sworn she heard a low masculine voice mutter, "Coward!"

She forced herself to ignore it and stepped outside.

"Maybe I am a coward," she murmured, to the surprise of a passing policeman and a scruffy dog. "He does frighten me in a way. But being a coward is a lot better than being a sacrificial lamb. Or a lemming bent on senseless self-destruction.''

Funny, though, she didn't feel any particular satisfaction now that there was no longer any possibility that she, Ashley Kalani, would become the latest in a long line of McGraw's conquests. In fact she felt exceptionally depressed.

But that would pass. It had to.

Frowning, she took the bus home. Maria was there complaining loudly about her latest boyfriend, and Gina was grumbling that she didn't like fish, and why couldn't she have hot dogs instead?

Everything was back to normal. And tomorrow she would see Mr. White at the corner store. He'd been trying to persuade her to work for him for months, and recently he'd almost offered to match Boyko's wages.

Things stayed normal until the following Friday, when Ashley was called to the university office and told to go at once to the hospital. Her brother Nick had been hit on the head with a puck while playing hockey. He was unconscious, and they didn't know if he would live.

No, she thought, as she climbed into the car that had miraculously been provided. Oh, no, not Nick! Please, God, please don't let him die. I'll never complain about his noisiness again, I really won't. He can make all the racket he wants. I'll even join him.

She continued to attempt futile bargains with the Almighty all the way to the hospital, and when she finally stepped into the elevator she began to think that her anxiety over her brother was driving her mad. Because just as the doors closed, she saw a man stride into the lobby. She closed her eyes, and when she opened them again there was nothing to see except the back of another passenger's head. She ran a hand over her damp forehead. It couldn't have been. Could it? What possible reason could Gray have for being here?

Nick was hooked up to an intimidating array of tubes and needles. Rosa and Toivo were already there, looking ashen and ten years older. Her father told her that when Nick had fallen he had also received a nasty gash on his neck, and had apparently lost a lot of blood.

Rosa was groaning softly as she stared at her gray-faced son lying bandaged and abnormally still against the sheets.

"Will he be all right?" whispered Ashley.

"They don't know," said Toivo. "He was wearing a helmet, but it shattered. One of those freak accidents that aren't supposed to happen." He blew his nose loudly and looked away. "They're keeping a close eye on him, though." He spoke with a desperate brightness that Ashley guessed was assumed mainly for her mother's benefit.

She felt a lump swell in her throat as she stared at the small, still figure. "Nick'll be all right," she said, "I know he will. He's always been a tough little nut, and he's not going to give up this easily. Mom . . . Dad, you have to believe that, you really do."

Toivo nodded. "That's right. Ashley's right, Rosa. He'll be fine—of course he'll be fine."

Not long afterward Ashley left to take care of the rest of the family, and again just as she was leaving she thought she caught a glimpse of Gray getting into a car. She blinked. It was possible, of course. But if he was visiting someone in the hospital, why hadn't he said so? It was very strange . . .

Her bus came then, and she forgot about Gray, as her mind returned to her brother.

Much later that night, an exhausted Ashley spoke to her father again, this time over the telephone.

"He's still asleep," said Toivo, who sounded utterly worn out and drained. "But they say he's going to come around. We should know for sure by tomorrow, but, please God, I think he's all right. Your mother and I are staying here."

"Yes, of course," said Ashley. "Don't worry, Dad, I'll look after the gang at home."

"I know you will, I know you will."

As Toivo hung up the phone, she could hear the sound of his nose being blown again—very noisily.

"Dad says they think Nick's going to be all right," she said to Sophia, Maria and Rocky, who were clustered around her in the hall.

The collective shout of relief that greeted this announcement made Ashley's eyes fill up yet again.

"Gee," said the irrepressible Sophia, recovering first, "for a while there I thought there might be one less of us to fight with over the bathroom." She sighed. "Ah, well, you can't win 'em all."

Ashley tried to look severe, but couldn't manage it, and a few minutes later, laughing, and almost light-headed with relief and optimism, the four of them made their way upstairs to bed.

It wasn't until she was pulling on her nightdress that for the first time that evening it occurred to Ashley that she hadn't even thought about, let alone asked about, Maria's first evening working at the shop.

"Did you see the fiend?" she asked now, too tired to care much about the answer.

"Fiend? Oh, you mean Gray. Yes, he came in to make sure I was all right. He was on his way to some charity dinner and he looked terribly expensive and impressive. But he was nice. Very considerate."

"Gray? Considerate?" Ashley felt sure she was going to choke. But she could well imagine that he looked impressive in evening clothes. She wondered what the occasion was, and if he had taken a partner...

"I don't know why you gave up that job, Ash," sighed her sister. "He's a dream!"

Suddenly Ashley found she wasn't as tired as she'd thought she was. "Dream? Maria, what's he been up to? He didn't..."

Maria frowned. "Didn't what?"

"I mean he didn't—that is, you're a pretty girl, and he's very attractive..."

"Oh," said Maria, "I see what you're getting at. No, he didn't, worse luck. He was just—nice."

Ashley shook her head. "I don't get it. *I'm* the one he wants to get into bed, but *you're* the one he's nice to."

Maria giggled. "I wish I thought it was because he's trying a new approach. But I'm afraid he just isn't interested."

"Maria! You're too young——"

"I'm eighteen. Mom was married at my age."

"Yes, and she'd have a fit if you tried to follow her example."

Maria giggled again.

"I'm going to sleep," said Ashley firmly. "You'd better do the same. I'm glad the job went okay, though."

"Mmm. It sure beat this evening. Poor old Nick!" As Maria pulled the covers up around her shoulders she added sleepily, "I forgot to ask—are you looking for a new job now, Ash?"

"Not any more. I'm starting at the corner store next week."

"Oh, that's great!"

Yes, thought Ashley as her eyes began to droop closed, I suppose it is great. I'll have a new job that won't pay quite as well—but at least the boss won't try to kiss me.

She frowned, wondering if she really had seen Gray this evening. But in spite of her suspicions, and not for the first time, she fell asleep on the memory of his kiss—warm, sensual, intoxicatingly seductive, like no other kiss she'd had before. And when she began to dream, it wasn't of her injured brother, but of a lean, tough man's body, dark hair curling on a man's neck, and eyes that were as deep and dark as Hades...

"Well, *you* sure gave us a scare, didn't you? How are you, Nick?"

It was the following Wednesday, and the first time Ashley had visited the hospital since her brother's accident. Rosa had been there almost constantly, while Ashley kept the household running, but tonight she was taking an evening off, in the hopes of getting some much needed rest.

Nick gazed up at his sister gloomily. "I guess I'm s'posed to be okay. But that stupid doctor says I can't play hockey again this season. And if I don't play, all the other guys will be better 'n me, and I'll *never* make it into the NHL. I've *got* to play, Ash!"

"You've got to stay alive," said Ashley dryly. "None of us wants to go through a week like this one again."

"Hell, you're as bad as Mom and Dad," Nick muttered, his lower lip protruding sulkily.

"Don't swear," said Ashley. Then she remembered she was supposed to be cheering him up, and made a valiant attempt to change the subject.

An hour later, when her time was up, she hurried into the corridor with a sigh of slightly guilty relief. Phew! she thought, mentally wiping her brow. The next few weeks *are not* going to be plain sailing!

The possibility of Nick taking his banishment from the ice lying down was about as likely as that of Gina getting through an entire meal without complaining.

She was so busy staring glumly at the sterile hospital floor, and thinking about the disgruntled child plotting rebellion in the room behind her, that she paid no attention whatever to her surroundings. When she stepped into the crowded elevator, she didn't so much as glance at the other passengers.

It wasn't until they reached the ground floor, and a firm hand closed around her elbow, that she finally bothered to look up—and in that moment she thought for a moment she must be dreaming. Because the eyes staring down into hers were the same ones that had invaded her sleep every night for the past week. And they belonged to the one man she had been determined to have absolutely nothing further to do with.

No, *not* a dream.

"More like a nightmare," she muttered, not realizing she was speaking out loud.

"What did you say?"

Oh, what the hell. "I said you were a nightmare," she repeated. There had never been much point in lying to Gray—and, anyway, she didn't want to.

"That's what I thought. A typically charming sentiment, my dear. Does that mean I've been haunting your dreams, then? How very promising!"

CHAPTER SIX

ASHLEY gasped. "I'm not promising you anything," she snapped. "And no, of course you haven't been haunting..." She hesitated a fraction too long. "You haven't been haunting my dreams."

"Liar."

"Oh, don't be so damn smug!" she shot back, furious that she'd given herself away, furious with Gray for knowing it, and quite unbearably aware of the feel of his large hand on her coat. Because he wasn't holding her gently; he was gripping her arm as if he thought she might try to make a run for it.

"I am not in the least smug. If I had any lingering tendencies in that line, they were beaten out of me very shortly after I met you."

"I doubt that," said Ashley, who couldn't imagine anyone beating anything out of Gray.

"So do I."

She glanced up suspiciously, thinking he was in a much better mood than the last time she had seen him, and expecting to see the usual mocking smile. Instead she encountered a steady dark gaze that made her feel uncomfortable and confused.

"What are you doing here?" she asked, attempting to defuse an awkward moment by sounding politely unconcerned.

To her surprise, her question was met with a look that was curiously guarded, and his face seemed to close up as if he had withdrawn into some private world of his own.

"Visiting," he replied curtly.

"Oh. A—a friend?"

"No," his jaw tilted at an aggressive angle, "not a friend."

"Oh," said Ashley again, deciding it would be unwise to press him further, but irritated by his persistent reticence. She guessed now where he had been going all along, so why the unreasonable taciturnity?

By this time they had reached the exit, and she tried to pull away from him. He wouldn't release her.

"What are you doing here, Ashley?" he asked gruffly.

Well, of all the nerve! she thought. He shuts up like a clam when I ask *him* that very same question, and then calmly turns around and demands the same information from me!

She glared at him, tempted to give him the answer he'd given her. But there wasn't much point. There was no deep dark secret about poor Nick's misfortune.

"My brother Nick had an accident," she informed him—a bit tartly. "On the ice. His helmet shattered."

A shadow passed over Gray's features. "Hell, I'm sorry. Is he okay?" The words were abrupt, but there was a look in his eyes that betrayed a feeling much deeper than mere polite concern for the brother of an ex-employee. Ashley remembered that he too had suffered an accident. An accident that had changed his life.

"Yes, he's okay," she replied slowly. "But he's going to be a problem."

"In what way?"

"He thinks he should be allowed to climb out of bed and skate right back on to the ice. The doctors say 'no way,' but Nick figures he'll never make the NHL if he doesn't get on skates again this year." She sighed. "I foresee a winter of discontent, with my poor mother forced to play jailer to my diabolically evasive brother—who will almost certainly manage to break out."

Gray, who no longer looked withdrawn and guarded, smoothed a hand hastily across his mouth before saying soberly, "I see. Obviously stern measures will have to be taken."

"Yes, but they won't be," said Ashley gloomily. "Dad's too softhearted, Mom's not much better, and all the rest of them will aid and abet him."

"Which leaves Ashley."

"Who's much too busy."

"Mmm, it is a problem," he agreed, finally releasing her arm. He ran a contemplative eye over her slim figure in its bright red coat. "*Are* you busy, Ashley? Have you found another, more desirable boss?"

"No," said Ashley without thinking. "Mr. White's not desirable at all. He's married, bald and too old for me." Then, as she realized what she had said, her hand flew to her mouth as her cheeks turned a bright scarlet that successfully rivaled her coat.

Gray made no effort at all to hide his amusement, and the gleam that lit his eyes was pure devil. "That wasn't precisely what I meant," he said softly, "but if you want to put it that way, as I'm neither married, bald, nor too old for you, I suggest you come back to work for me."

"Oh, stop it!" Ashley snapped sharply, knowing she'd walked right into that one. "You know I can't do that."

"I don't know anything of the sort."

"Well, I can't. You'll just have to settle for Maria."

"It's a thought, I suppose," he murmured, deliberately misunderstanding her. "She's very pretty. But, as I think I've already told you, she's a little too young."

"Oh, don't you dare even think it!" cried Ashley, her voice rising several octaves.

Two nurses hurrying through the door glanced at her in surprise, and then, catching sight of Gray, paused to give him a quick, approving once-over. He returned it with interest, and Ashley had to bite her tongue to prevent herself from saying something she knew she'd regret a second later. Something unprintable which, she recognized disgustedly, would be prompted more by jealousy than by any great concern for propriety in the hallowed hospital halls.

Gray turned back to study her bright-eyed, flame-colored face. "Think what?" he asked innocently.

"Don't pretend to be stupid, Gray McGraw. You keep your hands off my sister!"

"Certainly. I'd much rather keep them on you."

"And you can forget that as well. Now, if you don't mind, I have a bus to catch in a minute."

"Nonsense. I'll drive you."

"No, you won't."

"Just try and stop me."

"I certainly will stop you——" Ashley pushed her way past him and ran out into the night. She hadn't gone two steps before she felt his hand take her elbow again.

"Stop behaving like an idiot! It's cold, and my car's right here."

"Don't you tell me how to behave! And I'm taking the bus."

"All right, I won't. I'll show you. And you're not."

Without wasting any more words he swung her around, put his hands on her hips and slung her over his shoulder—as if she were no heavier than a child. She started to kick frantically, until the hand that wasn't wrapped around her thighs descended smartly onto her bottom and remained there.

"Keep still," he ordered.

After that Ashley couldn't do anything but keep still. Even through the thickness of her coat, the feel of his hands on her body, and the broadness of his back as she gazed down at it from this undignified angle, acted as an aphrodisiac to her senses. And it was icy cold and windy this evening. What his closeness would do to her in the heat of a summer night didn't bear thinking of. She groaned inwardly.

Not a moment too soon they arrived beside his car, and Ashley found herself dumped unceremoniously upright as Gray unlocked the door and told her to sit.

Fleetingly she thought about making a break for it, but it was almost a foregone conclusion that he would catch up to her, and her dignity had suffered enough for one evening.

With her small nose pointed very straight ahead, she did as he told her, and sat.

"Do you always behave like Ghenghis Khan?" she asked frostily, as he swung his long legs up beside hers.

"Rarely. And don't exaggerate."

Ashley pursed her lips and maintained what she hoped was a regal silence until the car pulled up in front of her parents' house. If she had troubled to glance at Gray's face, though, she would have been mortified to note that, far from him being offended by her attitude, his lips were parted in a broad, thoroughly self-satisfied grin.

She didn't even say "thank you" when he reached across to open the door for her, but she did wonder if he would have got out to hold it if he hadn't known she'd beat him to the draw.

To her consternation, when his fingers closed around the handle he didn't turn it. Gulping, she held herself rigidly against the back of the seat to minimize the pressure of his arm.

"Aren't you going to thank me?" he murmured. His face was so close to hers that she could feel his spicy breath on her cheek.

"For kidnapping me?" she exclaimed, in a voice that came out in a squawk.

"No, for driving you home. Say 'thank you' and I'll open the door."

"I will not!" snapped Ashley.

"Ah, then I'll have to extract a more stimulating form of thanks."

She jumped, as his head turned suddenly, and before she knew what was happening, his lips were brushing over hers and extracting, not thanks, but the beginnings of an unwilling response. Oh, dear, she thought as desire began to curl in her stomach. Oh, dear. Would she never be proof against the persuasive magnetism of this horribly overbearing man?

As soon as he felt her lips begin to open under his, Gray raised his head.

"You're a rat, Gray McGraw," she muttered, when at last he released the door. As the car filled with cold night air, she repeated angrily, "A complete rat!"

"No, I'm not. I'm a man who's just done you a favor. For which, in spite of yourself, you have given me quite ample reward."

"Oh," gasped Ashley. "Oh!" As she stumbled onto the street she turned to glare at him—only to see that he was laughing. His dark, handsome face, which could so often seem brooding and severe, was lit with a devilish amusement, and his wide white grin was pure pirate. Which was appropriate, she fumed irrelevantly. Because he'd kidnapped her...

"Oh," she said again. "You..." She gave up and swung away from him to stamp up the path to her door.

Behind her she heard a soft male chuckle purr with a soft seduction through the night. Then Gray called, "Good night, sweet Ashley," before switching on the engine of his car.

"Damn him," muttered Ashley, fumbling furiously for her keys. "Damn, damn, damn him!"

Had he only been teasing her, then? Was that what that had all been about, why he'd slung her over his shoulder like a caveman selecting his mate? Or did he really think he had the right? Partly he'd been getting his own back, she supposed, because he hadn't liked it when she had refused to work for him any longer. And he might have had a genuine impulse to rescue her from the cold and her own obstinacy. On the other hand, as he had once admitted, he enjoyed baiting her...

As she closed the door and listened to the TV blaring across the hall, reluctantly—very reluctantly—she began to smile. If baiting her had been his aim, then he had succeeded most brilliantly. She had fallen into his trap like a gullible fool. Shaking her head, she made her way thoughtfully upstairs, and slowly her reluctant smile turned into a gurgle of laughter. All right, so Gray had won this round. Next time—and for some reason she had a feeling now that there would be a next time—she wouldn't be such an easy mark.

When she went to bed that night, Ashley was surprised to find that for the first time in ages she didn't dream at all about Gray. But when she awoke in the morning she felt refreshed and lighthearted, and more ready than she'd been in weeks to face the day.

"Guess who came to visit me yesterday, Ash?"

It was Friday, Ashley had left college early, and Nick, well on the road to recovery, beamed up at her from under a somewhat reduced layer of bandage.

"I don't know, Nick. Who?"

"Someone important. Guess," he insisted.

Ashley's mind ran rapidly over a list of those likely to inspire that look of worshipful adoration on Nick's jubilant face.

Oh. Surely not...

"Batman," she said quickly, not wanting to hear what she had a sinking feeling Nick was about to tell her. "Or Darth Vadar."

"Silly! It was Gray McGraw." Nick's crow of triumph caused a passing intern to peer suspiciously at them around the door.

"Oh," said Ashley faintly. "That—that was nice of him."

"Yeah, and you know what? He brought me a whole pile of comic books. And he says I should do what the doctors say, and get well, and that I'll still have plenty of chances to play in the NHL. Even if I do miss a year."

"That's what I thought," said Ashley.

"Yeah, but Gray *knows*."

"God bless Gray McGraw," she muttered under her breath. And then she added glumly, "Damn him."

Why was it that Gray could arouse so many different feelings in her at the same time? Exasperation, gratitude, amusement, sometimes an outright urge to commit murder—and always, underlying every other emotion, there was desire. A desire she didn't want and couldn't cope with. Which was why she did her best to avoid him. Only her best wasn't very good, was it? Not when faced with his determination and, in this case, his kindness to her brother.

"Yes, Gray knows," she agreed with Nick. "I'm glad he's made you see sense."

Nick grinned and stuck out his tongue.

Ashley was still thinking about Gray, and wondering if she ought to phone to thank him, when she strolled out into the corridor an hour later. Just in front of her, an aide was walking past pushing a wheelchair.

She glanced down at its occupant—a man of about seventy with a shock of waving white hair—and immediately she stumbled, tripped over her own feet, then drew up with an audible gasp.

The man looked up without much interest, and Ashley gasped again. Her first stunned impression had been correct. This wasn't Gray who was staring at her with bright, intense dark eyes, but it was the spitting image of the way Gray might look forty years down the road. Tough, aggressive, a little leathery, still handsome—and very much in command of his world, even from the depths of a wheelchair. To think she had suspected Gray was visiting a woman!

"Mr. McGraw?" said Ashley tentatively. "It is Mr. McGraw, isn't it?"

The aide came to a reluctant halt as the occupant of the chair signaled imperiously at her to stop.

"Yup," said the man, in a deep, gruff voice that resembled Gray's but didn't have his distinctive drawl. "And who are you?"

"My name's Ashley——"

"Hah! Right. I know who you are. My boy's been muttering about you all week. Said you were a good worker, but a bloody infuriating woman. Why won't you go back to work for him, girl?"

"Because he's a bloody infuriating man."

Ashley saw his eyes register surprise, followed by a gleam of unwilling appreciation. Apart from that, his expression didn't change at all. "Hmm, you may be right there," he agreed. "That's the way I brought him up."

"So you're the one I should blame," said Ashley, smiling.

"Could be. You can't play to win without making some people mad."

"And is that all you brought him up to do? Play to win?"

The recognizably McGraw eyebrows bristled. "What's wrong with that? He had to have something, didn't he? Something to keep his name alive."

"Did he?" Ashley replied, puzzled, and wondering what had prompted the odd remark.

At this point the aide, who had been shuffling irritably, announced in a firm voice, "Mr. McGraw, I'm sorry to interrupt you, but we're very busy, and I have to get you back to your room."

Gray's father waved an impatient hand. "All right, all right, don't tell me your troubles. Hey, you! Come and talk to me." He raised his arm and beckoned to Ashley to follow.

For a moment she contemplated ignoring him. But he was apparently a sick man. He was also Gray's father, and just now she owed Gray a debt of gratitude for his pacification of Nick. Sighing, and with some trepidation, she followed the wheelchair down the hall, past the reception desk, and into a room very like her brother's.

"Would you like to get back into bed, Mr. McGraw?" inquired the aide.

"Nope. I'm not entertaining my boy's young lady in bed. He wouldn't like it." He gave Ashley a wolfish leer that reminded her painfully of his son. If there hadn't been a twinkle in his eye to belie the suggestive words, she might easily have been offended.

"I'm not Gray's young lady, Mr.——"

"Bruce," he interrupted. "I'm too young to be called Mr. McGraw."

The aide raised her eyebrows and hurried away, and Ashley perched awkwardly on the edge of the bed and smiled doubtfully down at Gray's surprising father.

"Bruce," she conceded. "But I'm still not Gray's young lady."

"Hmm. Why not? He wouldn't keep stomping around the house, swearing every time your name comes up, if he didn't have his eye on you, now would he? I know my boy."

"Yes," said Ashley, who knew him too, "I think he did have his eye on me..." And a lot more than his eye, she amended silently. "But that doesn't mean I have my eye on him. Gray's a—a very nice man—well, sometimes he is—but I don't want a man at the moment, Mr.—Bruce, and..."

To her surprise, Bruce McGraw's brows drew down in a scowl of impressive ferocity. "Huh!" he snorted. "So that's it. Holding out for a husband, are you?"

"What?" Ashley gaped at him, and felt a stirring of indignation at the same time as she felt her cheeks change color. Dammit, just because Gray's father was ill, that didn't mean he had the right to say anything that happened to come into his head. "No," she continued forcefully. "No, I am not holding out for a husband, Mr. McGraw. A husband's the very last thing I want at the moment, and, even if I did want one, I most certainly *wouldn't* choose your son!"

"Which," said a tightly furious voice behind her, "is just as well, isn't it? Because, for your information, if I were in the market for a wife, which I assure you I'm not, I certainly wouldn't choose you either, Ms. Kalani. Now get out!"

CHAPTER SEVEN

ASHLEY leapt up from the bed as if she'd been stung by an exceptionally dedicated wasp. Then she spun around quickly to face the man who, she suspected from the sound of his voice, was about to hurl her bodily out of the room.

"Gray!" she gasped, putting her hands behind her back and gripping the bedrail. "Gray, your father's ill——"

"My father's thoroughly enjoying himself," rasped Gray.

She stole a hasty glance at the man in the wheelchair. Gray was right. His black eyes were bright with amusement, and he was slapping his hand on his knee and muttering something which sounded like, "Go get her, boy!"

Ashley remembered what she'd heard about Gray wading in to collect any woman he wanted, if necessary using force. Only just at this moment she had a feeling that any force he might be inclined to use would *not* be employed in collecting her.

Dignity, she thought, swallowing. Hang on to your dignity, Ashley. It's the only hope.

"Very well," she said frigidly. "As our disinclination to marry—especially each other—seems mutual, it's a subject we won't bother to discuss." She turned to the alleged invalid, who was grinning hugely. "I've enjoyed meeting you, Mr.—Bruce, but as your son's here now——"

"Fat lot of good he is," interrupted Gray's father. "Look at him! Face like an unexploded bomb. It's enough to put a man off all that unhealthy hospital food." He threw a malicious little glance in Gray's direction. "Stay and keep me company, girl. I need someone cheerful around."

"I'm sure Gray will cheer you up once I've gone," said Ashley diplomatically.

"Fat chance," snorted Bruce. "With a face like that, he couldn't cheer up a jackass at a convention of clowns!"

Ashley stole a look at Gray. His father was right. Coal black eyes smoldered furiously, and his jaw was squared off like an ax. "Well..." she began doubtfully '...I'm sure——"

"So am I. Sure that you're leaving. Now." Gray took a step toward her, and Ashley, still determined to maintain her dignity, raised what she hoped was a supercilious eyebrow and didn't deign to reply.

Just for a moment Gray looked baffled, and then his jaw became even more axlike as he took another step, grabbed her arm, turned her around and propeled her purposefully toward the door.

Ashley glanced over her shoulder, smiled, and said brightly to Bruce McGraw, "Goodbye, Mr. McGraw. I hope we'll meet again before long. And I hope you'll soon be feeling better."

Gray's father gave another snort and the eyes that were so like Gray's gleamed delightedly. "I'll make sure of it," he called after her. "I like you, girl."

"Don't kid yourself," muttered Gray, still holding her arm and bending down to growl into her ear. "He may like you, but you're not getting anywhere near my father again. D'you understand?"

"Not really," said Ashley coolly, annoyed to find she liked the feel of his breath fanning over her ear. "I imagine that's up to him, isn't it?"

"Not if I have anything to do with it," said Gray, sounding exactly like the unexploded bomb his parent had called him.

"Really?" said Ashley sweetly. "But I don't see why you *should* have anything to do with it, do you?"

Gray swore. "I'm warning you," he threatened, in a voice that was rapidly becoming a roar. "Don't you——"

"Oh, for heaven's sake!" Ashley discovered she was losing patience as well as all interest in her dignity. "Stop behaving like Julius Caesar, Gray! It was you who said I'd make a lousy slave." She shook his hand off without difficulty because he made no attempt to restrain her, and marched off down the corridor without bothering to look back. But she couldn't avoid hearing his response, which most certainly would not have been printed in a family paper.

What in the world had been going on in that sanitized hospital bedroom? she wondered bemusedly, as the elevator bore her down to the ground floor. Gray had acted almost as if he suspected her of trying to poison his father. Or was he just mad because he'd heard her say she wouldn't want to marry a man like him?

But that didn't make a lot of sense, did it? Because Gray didn't want to marry her either. He had said so. Was his nose just out of joint, then, now that he'd finally met a woman who wasn't panting to get her hands on his fame and fortune? She shook her head. From what she knew of Gray that didn't seem very likely either. Unless he was so used to being the one who called the shots that it galled him to have the tables turned...

The doors slid open, and she stepped out into the lobby. If that was the case, she was glad she'd succeeded in puncturing his ego. *If* she had. Only that seemed about as improbable as everything else that had happened this afternoon. Gray's reaction to her presence in his father's room had been beyond the bounds of mere pique. And anyway, he had never appeared particularly addicted to pique. Short temper, bossiness and arrogance, yes. But not pique.

Ashley was still frowning when she clambered onto the bus. Of course the Great McGraw had always been uncommunicative about his private life, she reflected as she sank into a seat. But today's exhibition had been carrying things altogether too far. And she wasn't putting up with any more of it. She had half intended to phone him to thank him for his assistance with Nick, but there was no question of that any more. Nothing would induce her to phone him.

Her frown became a scowl, and, by the time she climbed off the bus, Ashley was in a thoroughly bad humor. On top of which, she had a raging headache and a totally illegal desire to commit bodily harm against the person of a prominent member of the Thunder Bay Sports Hall of Fame.

Her spirits hadn't improved much by the next day either, and it took all her willpower to keep the smile on her face as she served bread, milk and newspapers to an endless procession of customers, most of whom seemed to shop at Mr. White's because it gave them a chance to unload their troubles on whoever happened to be behind the counter. By six o'clock, when her shift ended, Ashley was beginning to feel she'd been hired under false pretenses. What Mr. White really needed was a trained psychiatrist. In fact at the moment she felt she could do with one herself, so unusually depressed was her state of mind. Nor was she under any illusions as to the cause of her uncharacteristic gloom.

It was Gray's extraordinary behavior of the day before that had reduced her to this sorry state. It had come so quickly after the unexpected relief and comfort she had felt when he turned up in her life again last Wednesday...

"Bloody man," she muttered, as she closed the door behind her and trudged off into the snow.

The wind slapped at her face, and her eyes were on the gray puddles of icy sludge at her feet, so she didn't notice the sleek white car pull up beside her until a door opened and an abrupt masculine voice said, "Hop in."

Ashley jumped, missed her footing and ended up facedown in the snowbank beside the road.

"For crying out loud!" exclaimed the same voice, more exasperated now than abrupt. "Can't you even stand on your own feet?"

As Ashley struggled to right herself, she felt two firm hands grasp her waist, and a moment later she was hauled upright to face the author of her current discomfiture.

"Who's a bloody man?" asked Gray interestedly, his dark eyes gleaming down at her damp, snow-crusted figure.

"You are," she said forthrightly, shivering as a trickle of sleet slithered down her back.

"You're maligning me again," he said mildly. "I came to give you a ride home."

"I don't need a ride home. I can walk."

"That's debatable," he observed, reaching beneath her collar and removing a handful of melting ice from her neck.

"Not to me, it isn't. Excuse me, Gray, I have to go."

"Nonsense. Get in the car."

"Gray," said Ashley, her lips tightening, as they so often did around him, "I am not accepting a ride from you. Please let me pass."

"No," said Gray.

For a few seconds they stood there, eyes locked in frozen combat. Then Gray said, "Oh, for heaven's sake," and without further ado picked her up and dumped her into the car. As she gasped and made to get out again, he slammed the door on her and locked it.

She was still struggling with the handle when he eased himself in beside her, leaned across her to fasten the seat belt, and, without a word, moved into first gear.

"Hey!" shouted Ashley. "You can't——"

"Yes, I can," he interrupted. "Just watch me."

Ashley clamped her mouth shut, determined not to give him the satisfaction of reacting. They'd be home in a minute anyway, and he couldn't hold her prisoner while they were parked directly in front of her parents' house.

She was right—he couldn't. But, as she soon realized they weren't heading anywhere near her parents' house, that fact wasn't much consolation.

"Where do you think you're taking me?" she asked furiously, unable to maintain a restrained silence any longer.

"I don't. I know where I'm taking you."

Ashley tried not to grind her teeth. "I suppose it's too much to ask you to share that knowledge with me?" she said icily.

"Mmm, in view of your thoroughly ungracious behavior, I rather think it is," he agreed blandly.

"My ungracious..." began Ashley. Then she relapsed into a glowering silence again, because, when she happened to look up, she saw that Gray was smiling. It was probably the most aggravating smile she had ever seen in her life.

All right, she thought malevolently. All right, Gray McGraw, you win this round too. But just you wait till the next time!

A few minutes later they pulled into the garage of a very large three-storeyed house on High Street with a

magnificent view of the lights of Thunder Bay. Ashley
blinked. So this was where Gray lived. She might have
known. On a street where most of the big turn-of-the-
century houses had been converted to apartments, Gray
and his father dwelt in lordly possession of more than
sufficient space to house a family and a number of
servants.

Ashley kept up her cool silence as Gray slid out of the
car and came around to open her door.

"Out you get," he said evenly.

She thought about refusing to move, but that hadn't
succeeded too well in the past, and in any case she stood
a much better chance of escaping him if she could get
her hands on a phone. Apart from which, wearing a
heavy dark overcoat, and with his fingers tapping impatiently on the roof, Gray looked very large and intimidating in the dim light of the spacious garage.

Ashley got out.

"Good girl," he said approvingly, as he took her arm
and led her into a narrow passageway leading to a big
modern kitchen decorated in warm earth tones that
beautifully complemented the polished copper pans on
the walls.

The instant they stepped through the doorway, they
were assaulted by what appeared to be a shaggy black
carpet with legs. And a tongue, amended Ashley faintly,
as two black paws descended onto her shoulders and a
moist pink appendage proceeded to cover her cold face
with wet kisses.

"Down, Daisy," ordered Gray.

Immediately the carpet, which was apparently called
Daisy, descended to the floor where it belonged. But
when it continued to gaze at her with chocolate colored
eyes that would have melted the snow off Mount Everest,
in spite of herself Ashley had to smile.

"That's Daisy," explained Gray, noting the smile.

"So I gathered."

Ashley wasn't Mount Everest and she wasn't melting that easily.

"She's my father's dog," he went on, ignoring her frostiness. "He found her in front of the fire eating his slippers when he left the door open one spring day about three years ago. So he lit the fire, exchanged the slippers for a steak, and Daisy, who knows a good deal when she sees one, has been here ever since."

"Couldn't you find her owners?" asked Ashley, not wanting to respond to him, but intrigued by the over-affectionate carpet who had succeeded in worming her way into the heart of a crusty old man.

"Yes, but they didn't really want her. That's why she ran away and categorically declined to go back."

"Smart dog," said Ashley, bending down to scratch Daisy's ecstatic head.

"She is," agreed Gray. "Almost as smart as you'd be if you stopped dog worshiping and got out of that wet coat." As if to make his point, he removed his own coat and slung it over a chair. Ashley saw that he was wearing black again, and quite unconsciously she licked her lips.

"I'm not dog worshiping," she said loftily, although that was exactly what she was doing. She'd always wanted a dog or cat, but, in a smallish house full of energetic Kalanis, she had been forced to concede that her parents had a reason for saying "No pets."

"You could have fooled me," said Gray, who hadn't missed the softer look on her face. "Come on, take your coat off."

"But I'm not staying," said Ashley, looking him straight in the eye. "My parents are expecting me for supper."

"No, they're not. I told them you were having it with me."

"But you had no right——"

"I make my own rights, as it happens."

Yes, that was what Jack had said, wasn't it? Although Gray was speaking quite mildly, without emphasis, the dark eyes fixed on hers left her in no doubt that he expected to win this battle as easily as he'd won so many other battles in his life. Except the one that mattered most, she remembered, with an irritating pang of sympathy.

"Don't fight me," he said now, softly and as if he'd read her mind. "See, it's all ready." He waved at the glass-fronted oven from which savory smells were floating. "I've hired a housekeeper recently, much to my father's disgust. *He* may be quite content to potter about cooking up unpleasant messes for himself, but I'm not. I assure you Mrs. Green's an excellent cook. She's also out this evening." He smiled obliquely.

"I'm not hungry," said Ashley, who was starving.

"In that case I wouldn't dream of forcing you to eat."

"Why not? You forced me to come here," she said resentfully. "I think you must be a frustrated buccaneer. This is the second time you've kidnapped me, Gray McGraw."

"Frustrated, certainly," he agreed dryly. "But hardly a buccaneer. Although I've been called worse names."

"I'll bet," snorted Ashley.

Gray shook his head reprovingly. "I kidnapped you because I had to," he said, as though that explained everything. "Now, take your coat off. You're shivering, and, as I *am* extremely hungry, I have no intention of taking you home until I've eaten. You can watch me," he added magnanimously.

Ashley glowered, but it was true she was cold and wet, and apparently he *did* intend to take her home eventually. When he stepped up beside her to ease the coat off her shoulders, she didn't resist.

Nor, for a reason which was beyond her, did she resist when, after flinging her coat down on top of his, he came over and placed both hands on her waist.

He didn't kiss her. Instead he stood staring down at her, his thumbs gently kneading her hips, and there was a curious look in his eyes as he studied her that left Ashley feeling thoroughly breathless and confused. It was a thoughtful look, revealing little, and yet she had a feeling he was displeased about something. And although she suspected she had something to do with his displeasure, she knew she wasn't really the cause.

After a while he drawled softly, and with just the faintest trace of a smile, "I could be persuaded to assuage a rather different kind of hunger. What do you think?"

Ashley, who not for the first time had been partly mesmerized by his eyes, found herself coming back to earth with a thud.

"No!" she cried. "Gray, I've told you already, I'm not interested in——"

"I know you have, but I'm not sure you're telling me the truth."

"Why?" She pushed his hands away and stepped back. "Because you can't believe you're not irresistible?"

He sighed. "Haven't we been over this before? No, Ashley, not because I think I'm irresistible. But do give me credit for noticing when a woman responds to me. I'm not above being flattered."

"I don't respond to you. I told you, I haven't time for that sort of thing."

Impatience flickered in Gray's eyes before they turned blank again. "All right," he said shortly. "You're not attracted to me, you didn't enjoy it when I kissed you, and you've never even considered going to bed with me. Is that right?"

Ashley's gaze slid away from his. "No," she replied in a tight voice, "you know it isn't. I *have* thought about going to bed with you. And thinking about it has sometimes had a disastrous effect on my concentration. Intermediate decision making wasn't designed with that sort of decision in mind. But I have made up my mind, Gray, and I'm not going to change it."

She glanced at him a little warily, and, to her amazement, saw that he was smothering a smile. "Fair enough," he conceded. "I'd hate to be found guilty of interfering with your concentration. So let's return to our original game plan, shall we? I'll eat, and you can sit down and watch."

Without wasting any more words, he withdrew the steaming casserole from the oven, and jerked his head at the door. Ashley, with no other option, followed him into a high-ceilinged room containing a long, rosewood dining table and a tall sideboard filled with what appeared to be antique silver. She was surprised to see that one whole wall was a bookcase, and that its volumes appeared to be mainly of a classical persuasion. Well-read classics too, she noted with further surprise. These books were not just decorations.

Gray didn't look at her as he deposited the casserole on a mat, pulled up a chair, and waved her to the one opposite. But he proceeded to serve himself a generous portion of what to Ashley's famished senses smelled like ambrosia fit for the gods.

She ran her tongue across her lips, unknowingly imitating Daisy, who was sitting at attention concentrating on Gray's plate with the apparent intention of hypnotizing its contents into her mouth.

He glanced up, caught the movement of Ashley's tongue, and said conversationally, "This is very good."

"Is it?" She sought desperately for something to take her mind off food. "Um—this is a big house for three people," she blurted, inanely stating the obvious.

"I suppose it is. But having spent a lot of my life in hotel rooms, I decided I wanted space. My father wanted this place, so I bought it. It was a fair bet I'd eventually end up living in my old home town."

Ashley would have thought it was a fair bet he'd eventually end up living somewhere larger, with more opportunity to make his presence felt. But she didn't say so, because her attention was riveted on the meal which Gray continued to consume with ostentatious enjoyment.

Swine! fumed Ashley, trying not to betray a fascination with his plate that rivaled Daisy's. He might at least give me another chance to refuse. She fidgeted with a much-too-clean fork and realized that a place had been set for her. Of course there was nothing to stop her asking if she could join him, but she was damned if she was swallowing her pride to that extent. Not after he had deliberately abducted her.

Gray finished his meal with a flourish and casually helped himself to more. When that was gone too he put down his knife and fork, leaned back in his chair, looked up at her—and burst out laughing.

"What's so funny?" she asked sourly.

"You are. I wondered if you'd be able to keep it up— and you did. Congratulations." His voice was still shaking with laughter.

"Congratulations on what?" Ashley frowned suspiciously.

"On enduring the sight of me enjoying that wonderful meal you were just dying to help me out with. I could practically hear your mouth watering."

"It wasn't..." she began. Then she closed her eyes. Who was she trying to kid? She *was* starving. And she had refused his invitation out of sheer bloody mindedness because she objected to his high-handed method of getting her here. She had every right to object, too. On the other hand, she also had a right to eat, and the only person she was hurting by her refusal was herself.

And Gray continued to look disgustingly smug.

Ashley sighed. "I suppose you think I'm a total idiot," she said resignedly.

"Not more than usual. But I'm enormously impressed by your willpower."

"Obstinacy," she corrected him wryly. "And now, having proved your point, do you suppose I could have some of that cold casserole?"

"Of course you could. And it won't be cold—I'll put it in the microwave. I'm not altogether a monster, Ashley. Did you really think I'd let you starve?"

She noted that his voice was practically caressing her now, warm and smooth and seductive. "Yes," she admitted, "I thought you were quite capable of it."

"Mmm." He stood up. "Under some circumstances I would be, but not in this case." He left the room abruptly.

"Why not in this case?" she asked, when he came back carrying the reheated casserole.

"Because I didn't bring you here to torture you, believe it or not. I realize you think I'm Torquemada reincarnated, but I mean to change that. It doesn't do a thing for my ego." He leaned over and began to load her plate with enough food to overwhelm an Amazon.

"Not Torquemada," said Ashley, her eyes glazing over at the sight of the savory feast he had placed before her. "Blackbeard."

He rubbed a hand around the back of his neck. "Blackbeard?"

"The pirate. You kidnapped me, didn't you?"

He suppressed a smile. "Not at all. I merely exercised a little persuasion."

"Persuasion!" scoffed Ashley. "If that's your idea of persuasion——"

"It isn't really. On the other hand, I felt some kind of pressure was required in order to get your attention."

Not likely, thought Ashley. He'd never had trouble getting her attention. That was the problem.

"I doubt it," she said dryly. "But I suppose I might have refused to come. Anyway, now that you've got me where you want me, what's the agenda?"

"Oh, I haven't by any means got you where I want you," he said, his sexy baritone so soft and suggestive that she lowered her eyes. "But that we'll leave until later." He moved over to the sideboard and came back with a bottle of wine. "For now I'll settle for conversation."

"Decent of you," muttered Ashley.

Gray grinned. "Isn't it?"

Ashley took her time swallowing a delicious morsel of Mrs. Green's excellent casserole. "Gray," she said severely, "after that deplorable exhibition at your father's bedside, can you think of one single reason why I should talk to you?"

He winced. "No, I can't. That's why—well, partly why—I brought you here. I can't take back what I said yesterday, Ashley, but I can promise it won't happen again."

"It certainly won't," agreed Ashley, not at all sure she liked the sound of his "partly."

Apparently that wasn't the reply Gray had expected. "What does that mean?" he asked, frowning.

"It means you won't be getting the opportunity to play emperor to my slave again, that's all. I don't work for you any longer, I don't intend to be so careless as to let you abduct me again, and I see no reason why our paths should ever cross. Do you?" She fixed him with a look every bit as steely as any he was capable of producing, even at his most autocratic.

For answer Gray removed the cork expertly from the wine bottle and leaned across the table to fill her glass. "Mmm," he said, not hurrying his reply. "As a matter of fact, I do. Your sister's a big help in the shop, and so is the young fellow I've hired to replace the lamentable Jack—but I want you back, Ashley. The—customers miss you." He smiled with a certain irony. "So, apparently, does Mrs. Cartwright."

So that was why she was here. She bit her lip, exasperated to discover that she had to squelch an annoying stab of disappointment. Then she saw that Gray was watching her with bland and carefully cultivated innocence. She choked. "If that piece of news is supposed to lure me back," she gasped, trying with limited success not to laugh, "I can only say that as a salesman you'd be a disaster."

"I know." He shrugged unconcernedly. "The truth is, I'm not used to selling. I'm used to telling people what I want and, in most cases, getting it."

"Well, you're not going to get what you want in this case," she retorted, with what she recognized guiltily was a feeling of juvenile triumph.

Gray refilled the glass she hadn't even realized she'd half finished, and Ashley chewed another delicate mouthful of the casserole she was dying to gulp down whole.

"Aren't I?" he replied, lowering himself back into his chair. He stared at her speculatively across the table.

"No."

"Hmm." He tapped his fingers on the smooth wood, and after a few moments of total silence seemed to come to a decision. "Perhaps you're right. You interfere with my concentration too, and I still have my hands full at head office—not to mention some of the shops. Charlie

Boyko left quite a mess, I'm sorry to say, and the staff are in need of a firm hand."

"The sort of hand you gave Jack?" she suggested, resurrecting an old grievance. "Are you going to fire *everyone* before Christmas?"

"For goodness' sake, Ashley!" His brow creased with impatience. "If you must know, that young man is a damn sight better off where he is—under the watchful eye of Joe Chernyk, where he won't get a chance to slack off. Having to do an honest job of work for a change won't do him any harm at all. I couldn't be around enough myself to get him properly licked into shape."

Ashley's eyes narrowed. There was something about what he'd said that made her wonder... "Does that mean *you* got him the job at the supermarket?" she demanded, her eyes accusing.

"Guilty," said Gray briefly, the dismissive wave of his hand indicating that he didn't wish to discuss the subject further. "Now stop trying to pretend you have the appetite of a bird, which you obviously haven't, and finish your dinner."

Ashley was so busy digesting the surprising revelation that Gray had not, after all, been quite as ruthless with Jack as she'd imagined, that she obeyed him without taking in that she was doing it.

"Well, that's a start," he said when she had finished.

She looked up, startled.

"What is?"

"Getting you to do what you're told."

She gazed at her empty plate, and then at him. "It was an accident."

"Mmm, I was afraid it might be."

Ashley frowned, not trusting this unexpected mildness. "What was it a start of?" she asked suspiciously.

"My campaign to seduce you, of course."

He was leaning back in his chair, casually twirling his glass as if he had just come up with the most natural suggestion in the world. And Ashley had no idea whether he was teasing her or not.

"I can't think why you imagine it's likely to succeed," she said dryly. "That little scene yesterday was hardly the standard prelude to seduction."

"Ouch!" He made a face. "No, put like that, I suppose, it wasn't."

She stood up, knocking a fork against her glass and making it sing. "You're not even going to bother to make excuses, are you?" she accused him.

"No. I can't think of any."

"I'm not surprised," muttered Ashley. She put both hands on the table. "How about an explanation, then?"

"I told you, there isn't an explanation."

"No, you told me there wasn't an excuse."

His mouth twisted. "Same thing. Either way, I agree that it was unacceptable behavior."

Ashley certainly concurred with him on that score. She also wondered why his eyes, which for a while there had reflected something that might have been remorse, as well as a rueful self-mockery, had suddenly turned bleak and rather hard. "It is not the same thing, and you know it," she retorted.

"Isn't it? I guess you're right."

"Well?" she demanded. Dammit, he owed her something—some kind of justification for his behavior.

Gray said nothing for a long time, and she observed that his jaw had tightened perceptibly and that he was staring blankly into space.

"I sincerely regret what happened," he said finally, expressing the words formally, without emotion. "But there isn't an explanation—any more than there's an excuse. You'll have to accept that, I'm afraid."

"I don't actually have to accept anything," she retorted, pressing her knuckles against the polished wood. "Not that it really matters, does it, as I won't be seeing you after today."

Contrarily, now, she regretted the truth of that statement.

But to her confusion, Gray returned from whatever private space he'd been inhabiting, and smiled. It was precisely that lazy, melting smile that in the past had always had the effect of making her do exactly what he wanted.

Today was no exception.

"Certainly you'll be seeing me," he said easily. "How about tomorrow? My father won't be home till next week, and I can send Mrs. Green to the movies. She'll be delighted."

Ashley gaped at him. He couldn't be serious. "I can't," she said quickly. "Mom spends a lot of time at the hospital with Nick, and she needs me at home to help, and I've got exams, and really——"

"You're babbling," he interrupted softly. "Shut up."

Ashley shut in midsentence. He was right—she was babbling. Because she was afraid that, if she didn't, she'd agree to do as he asked. Which would be disastrous, insane and plainly asking for trouble.

"That's better," said Gray, rising slowly and resting his palms on the table. "Now, as I was saying, how about we settle on tomorrow?"

His smile was so disarming, so sexy and so devastatingly persuasive that again, to her own disbelieving disgust, Ashley found herself giving in.

"All right," she mumbled ungraciously.

As soon as the words were out of her mouth she knew she'd made a mistake. Gray was trouble. Not only because he could distract her from her appointed path with unnerving ease, and probably in more ways than one, but because there was something about him she just didn't understand. Something controlled and guarded and disquieting. His strange behavior at the hospital was only part of it.

She rubbed a finger abstractedly around the edge of her plate. It was too late now, though, she had already committed herself. And Gray had his back to her and was heading briskly into the kitchen.

Ashley picked up her plate and followed him. "Thank you for talking sense into Nick," she said hastily, lighting on what she hoped was a nonthreatening topic. Then she swallowed, as her bemused gaze lit on a vision of Gray's seductively upthrust backside. He was scraping leftovers into Daisy's dish. When he straightened, and caught the look on her face, he raised his eyebrows and gave her an unmistakably suggestive grin.

Ashley, busy fighting back a blush, didn't move fast enough as Daisy, ears flying, came sliding from the far reaches of the house at the magic sound of food hitting plastic.

"Good grief!" exclaimed Gray, as the excited dog almost knocked Ashley flying, and he caught at her arm to hold her upright. "You're at it again! How on earth do you manage with those expanses of shiny floor at the university? Or do you spend most of the time flat on your——?"

"I cope very well," interrupted Ashley haughtily, flushing because the touch of his fingers was sending heated signals up her arm. She took a deep breath. "Gray, I said thank you for your help with Nick. It—it was very good of you."

Gray shrugged and released her arm. "No problem. I happened to be passing."

"With a pile of comic books?" she inquired dryly.

He shrugged again. "Nick's a nice kid. I kind of took to him."

Ashley studied him reflectively. "He took to you too. You're good with kids, aren't you? I ran into Mrs. Dalton the other day, and she said the terrible twins are reformed characters since they started coming over here to work for you. She even said they look forward to it."

He grimaced. "Wish I could say the same. They're not so bad when you get to know them, but their enthusiasm needs a lot of curbing. I was only just in time to prevent them painting my bedroom bright orange after they found an old tin of latex somewhere and thought they'd give me a—I suppose you'd call it a blinding surprise."

Ashley laughed. "You'll make a good father some day," she teased him, not wanting to pursue the subject of his bedroom any further.

She expected an equally flippant response, but, to her astonishment, his face turned dauntingly blank, and he stared at her as if she'd suggested he'd make an excellent child molester.

"Don't be ridiculous," he said coldly. "Don't you women ever think of anything except getting married— and producing packs of damp, revolting brats?"

CHAPTER EIGHT

ASHLEY'S mouth fell open. "What?" she murmured, stunned. "Gray, I only said you'd make a good father some day. Not that I wanted to get married, and certainly not that I wanted to produce kids." When he turned his back on her and didn't answer, she continued doggedly, "Besides, you don't mean a word of it. You *like* kids. Probably even better than I do."

His shoulders moved irritably under the black shirt, but he still said nothing. Ashley felt her temper rising.

"Are you by any chance suggesting that I have personal designs on you?" she inquired icily. "Because I assure you nothing could be further from the truth."

That did produce a response. "So you've already mentioned," he said tightly, "and I can assure you that if it was ego gratification I wanted I certainly wouldn't look for it from you."

"Just as well," muttered Ashley, frowning at his much too stimulating back, and wondering what in the world had got into him now. He was such a study in contrasts. Self-assured and relaxed a lot of the time, and yet he could turn into an arrogant iceberg in the middle of a casual conversation or a sentence, and apparently for no reason whatever.

"Gray," she said, in the kind of voice her friends knew meant that she intended to have an answer, "just what is it you *do* want? You dragged me here against my will, gave me no explanation and very little in the way of apology for your atrocious behavior in the hospital, practically demanded that I go out with you tomorrow,

121

then started accusing me of having matrimonial designs. Which must mean either that you're crazy—or else that you think I am."

Instead of eliciting the scathing response she anticipated, this speech caused Gray to swing around to face her—and to her amazement he was wearing an expression of wry, half-guilty regret.

"I surrender," he said, lifting his hands above his shoulders. "Because I have to admit you have a point. I brought you here, in part, to make amends. And you're quite right, I haven't made a very good job of it." The unaccustomed experience of having to admit he was wrong had deepened the naturally low timbre of his voice so that it came out almost as a growl. "What I said about women and kids—I didn't mean it personally." He fixed his eyes grimly on the row of copper saucepans on the wall. "Sometimes I say things..." He broke off. "I guess you'll just have to put up with me."

"It's hard not to put up with being kidnapped," said Ashley dryly. "But I assure you I don't intend to put up with any more of it."

"I don't expect you to. Believe it or not, abducting helpless females who keep falling flat on their noses is not normally one of my specialities."

"I may be female," said Ashley indignantly, "but I'm not helpless. And I don't keep falling flat on my nose."

"No, but if I'd mentioned your charming bottom I was afraid you'd hit me." He rested a hip casually on a corner of the gold-tiled counter.

She considered hitting him—seriously—then thought better of it. "I may yet," she said caustically. "But if you'll condescend to explain your Jekyll and Hyde tendencies for once, I'll reconsider. Or is that too much to ask?"

She saw his lips compress briefly, but when he opened his mouth for a moment she believed he meant to let the wall he had built around himself crumble. Then his face closed up again, assuming the flat mask she had come to expect whenever he was asked for explanations.

"Yes," he said bluntly, "I'm afraid it is. And I suppose you won't believe me if I promise you I'll be pure Jekyll from now on?"

She sighed. "Can you think of any reason why I should?"

"Not really," he admitted, with irritating candor.

"So where do we go from here?" asked Ashley. "I know I said I'd see you tomorrow——"

"But you're thinking of changing your mind. Is that it?"

"Well..."

"Forget it. You're not changing anything." He put his hands in his pockets and tilted his head back, managing to look aggressive and disarming at the same time.

"Is that so?" Ashley put her hands on her hips. "And just how do you propose to stop me?" She was still confused, but not so confused that she was about to let him push her around.

"I can think of several ways," he replied, smiling now as his eyes ran over her with a slow, suggestive contemplation that made her body feel as if it were being basted. "But on the whole I think this will prove the most effective."

"What...?" began Ashley, wondering how he could change from smiling penitent to predator so fast. Then she stopped wondering as Gray closed the gap between them with astonishing speed, locked both arms around her waist and pulled her against him.

For a few seconds he just held her, so that she could feel his heartbeat through the fabric of his heavy black shirt. Then, with tantalizing slowness, he lowered his mouth over hers, and kissed her with all the devastating, unbearable expertise that she had grown to expect of this man. And just as they had on those other occasions, her own needs soared to meet his in a way that was both exhilarating and frightening. After a while she slipped her hands around his shoulders and caught her fingers in the thick hair stroking his neck.

His kiss deepened, and everything in her began to cry out frantically for more.

And then it happened.

In one incredible flash of illumination, she knew that what she had been trying so hard to avoid had come to pass.

Desperately her tongue explored the soft recesses of his mouth as their lips pressed together, twisted, seeking the ever more intoxicating drug of an experience that was like nothing she had ever known. And of course what she did know, in the most secret part of her being, was that she had fallen in love with Gray McGraw. Now, whatever fate might have in store for her, her life could never be the same again.

Gray's hands were on her hips, rocking her against him. She couldn't fail to be aware of what she was doing to him, but when her palms slid under his shirt and she began to press her nails into his skin, he gave a long sigh, moved his hands back to her waist and held her away.

Ashley stared at him, her vision still misted with desire.

"Why...what?" she mumbled, bemused and incoherent, and not sure what was happening to her any more.

"Still want to break that promise, Ashley?" he asked softly. The lights in his dark eyes were making her head spin, and she didn't know what she wanted any more. As long as she didn't lose him.

"No." She shook her head, not sure what she was saying, and not caring. "I don't want to break any promises. What promises?" she added, as some semblance of common sense began to return. "What did I promise?"

Gray laughed, but it was a soft sort of laugh and this time not frightening at all. "It's too soon, isn't it?" he said quietly. "And I've been too much of a bastard. But I have plenty of time on my hands for once. I can wait. And it's all right—you only promised to go out with me tomorrow, nothing more. I just wanted to be sure you didn't have any foolish notions of backing out."

"Would you kidnap me again if I did?"

"Of course. And that would be the least of your worries."

"Oh." She thought about that. But it didn't really matter, did it? She wasn't thinking of backing out. How could she, now that she knew she loved him? She twisted the only button on his black shirt that was still done up, and sighed inwardly. Where all this was leading she had no idea. Probably to his bed and no further, and perhaps that was as it should be...

In her mind she saw her peaceful rose-covered cottage slipping rapidly into the never-never-land of forgotten dreams, and she made a frantic effort to grab it back. She wasn't sure if she'd succeeded, though, because Gray was patting her casually on the bottom, lifting his impossible eyebrows and asking, "Well?"

"Well what?" she gulped.

"Well, are you still thinking of backing out?"

He knew she wasn't. She could see it in the triumphant angle of his head, and in the confident slant of his mouth. But she gave him the answer he wanted.

"No, I'm not thinking of that. I'll see you tomorrow."

Daisy, who was stretched out on a bright woven mat watching them with her puzzled chocolate eyes, began to slap her long, feathery tail rhythmically up and down on the floor.

"She approves," said Gray, smiling as if he'd expected no other answer—as indeed he hadn't, she acknowledged ruefully.

Ashley moved away from him and began to collect the dishes for the dishwasher. Then she hesitated. "These plates," she said. "They're awfully expensive. What does Mrs. Green——?"

He shrugged. "I've no idea. The only thing I'm sure of is that she'd serve me broiled and buttered for breakfast if I broke one."

Ashley giggled at the idea of anyone broiling and buttering Gray. But she put the plates hastily back on the counter. If he was content to leave things to Mrs. Green, then so was she. Especially as he had already left the kitchen. Obviously Gray liked nice things, she mused with a certain surprise. But he didn't seem to regard their upkeep as his concern.

When he returned, he had a man's heavy gray parka across his arm.

"Here," he said, "put this on."

"But——"

"It's cold out, and your coat's still wet. Come on, it'll soon be your bedtime, won't it?"

"Yes, but..."

"Ah." His eyes gleamed. "You weren't by any chance about to remark that ''tis very warm weather when one's in bed?'"

"No, I was not! And neither were you. That's Swift, isn't it?"

"Mmm—well done. All right, to put it in more modern language, would you, by any chance, care to share my bed?"

When she only gulped, he heaved an exaggerated sigh and said, "That's what I thought. You'd prefer to sleep in your own."

She wouldn't, actually, but she wasn't telling him that. This whole situation needed a lot of thinking over, and leaping before she looked wasn't something she was in the habit of. Especially not when the leaping happened to involve this particular man's bed.

She nodded, and obediently put on the parka, which, Gray informed her tactfully as he zipped it up, made her look like an orphaned hippo. A few minutes later they were speeding through the darkened streets to her home.

Gray didn't kiss her again as he helped her out of the car, but before he left her on the step he bent forward suddenly, cupped her face in his hands, and ran his gloved thumb lightly down her nose.

"Good night, Ashley," he said, his deep voice warm and full of promise. "Until tomorrow."

She smiled dazedly. "Yes, until tomorrow." Then, rallying, she added quickly, "But leave Mr. Hyde at home."

"Absolutely," he agreed, very soberly.

Her parents were half-asleep in front of the television, and Maria wasn't home when she reached her room. Ashley hurried to the window and was in time to watch Gray take off rather fast into what appeared to be the beginnings of a fresh installment of snow.

She lay awake for some time, trying to make sense of the startling but, if she were honest, not entirely unexpected change in her relationship with her ex-boss. In a few short weeks her feelings about him had reversed dramatically. She had started out thinking of him as a rude customer. Then he had become her boss. From that, eventually, had grown a wary friendship, followed by an equally wary case of desire. Now the slate had been wiped clean again, because she knew, with no shred of doubt, that she was in love with this difficult, puzzling but utterly fascinating man. He was contradictory and arrogant and incurably reticent about his family. But he was also charming and capable, and startlingly well read for a man who had spent most of his life on the ice. He was gentle, too, when he wanted to be, and kind to animals and children. As well, she understood instinctively, he was vulnerable in some way she couldn't begin to comprehend.

Yes, she thought, as she heard Maria's key in the front door, Gray was all those things, and she loved him in spite of and because of them. But that didn't mean she knew what to do about him. He had no interest in marriage, of course, and just now she wasn't sure she had either. Marriage to Gray would never bring the peace and quiet she had dreamed of, and the only other alternative was an affair, which was apparently what he was working up to. But...

"It's exactly what I've never wanted," she whispered to the empty room.

"What is?" The room wasn't empty after all.

Ashley blinked as Maria flicked on the light. "An affair," she replied, without thinking.

"What?"

Realizing what she'd just said, Ashley struggled to a sitting position. "No, I don't mean... Listen, for God's sake don't tell anyone I said that. They'd all get the wrong idea—especially Dad."

"What do you take me for?" sniffed Maria. "Sophia?"

Ashley laughed. "You've got a point there. Don't be offended."

"All right..." Maria's indignation subsided "...so who are you having an affair with? Not Gray McGraw?" Her eyes were two hopeful black saucers.

Ashley sighed. "I'm not having an affair with anyone." She hesitated, then added honestly, "But I'm thinking about it."

"You think too much," said Maria, tossing her blouse over a chair. "If I had the chance to hop into that gorgeous man's bed, I wouldn't think for two seconds."

"Maria!"

"Well, I wouldn't." Her sister's tone was defiant.

"Oh," said Ashley, wishing she hadn't encouraged Maria to take on her old job at Boyko's, "does that mean you've actually...? I mean, have you——? Are you——?"

"Am I a fallen woman?" Maria giggled. "Not yet, but just give me time."

Ashley groaned. "It's not a game, Maria. Don't you realize——?"

"Of course I do, but, don't worry, I do intend to marry the man, whoever he happens to be."

"Whoever he happens to be?" repeated Ashley faintly.

"Yes—well, I mean I'd have to love him, wouldn't I?"

"But you said——"

"That I'd grab Gray if I thought I had a chance? Yes, but you see I know I *haven't* a chance, so I wouldn't let myself fall in love with him, would I?"

"Wouldn't you?" This was all getting too much for Ashley.

"Of course not. But you *are* in love with him, aren't you? So that's different."

Maria was more perceptive than she seemed, and Ashley didn't bother to deny the breezy assumption. "He's not in love with me, though," she exclaimed, knowing the truth had to be faced.

"Oh, I wouldn't be so sure about that," Maria replied airily. "I've seen the way he looks at you, you know."

"That's not love."

"Could be, though. Along with the other thing." Maria giggled and pulled on her nightgown. Ashley glared at her, speechless.

"Night, Ash," said her sister cheerfully. She switched off the light. "Sweet dreams—of Gray, I hope."

But Ashley didn't dream of anything, or, if she did, she didn't remember. It was hours before she finally fell asleep, still trying to decide what she meant to do about the future—about Gray. In the end she only knew that, with no real cause for it, she felt happy. She hadn't realized love would be like this.

Gray had said he would pick her up at one. At twelve-thirty, after a morning spent trying to study over the noise of Rocky's music, Rosa's vacuum cleaner and Gina's and Carlo's squabbling, Ashley gave up and decided she'd better settle on something to wear.

It was the usual problem, and, to make it worse, Gray hadn't said what they would be doing. Still, in the middle of the afternoon it couldn't be anywhere very fancy. She settled on black pants, a royal blue sweater and her bright red parka.

Sophia, who had never believed in minding her own business, was hovering in the hallway when she went down, which made Ashley doubly anxious to get away. She seized Gray's hand the moment he arrived and almost dragged him out to the car.

"What was the rush?" asked Gray, as he fastened her seat belt. "Afraid your sister might reveal the shocking secrets of your past? Or couldn't you wait to get me to yourself?"

"Neither," said Ashley dampingly. "If you must know, I was saving you from the clutches of the family matchmaker. Sophia has always fancied herself as Cupid. You should be grateful I dragged you away."

"Oh, I am." His eyes were on the road, and she couldn't tell from his profile whether he was serious or not.

"Where are we going?" she asked, wondering why she felt vaguely resentful.

"I thought we'd have some lunch first, then go up to visit young Nick. After that perhaps we might go skating."

Ashley smiled. It sounded like the perfect afternoon. "That would be lovely," she agreed. "It's thoughtful of you to think of visiting Nick." She took a deep breath. "What about your father? Shouldn't we visit him as well?"

The eye she could see didn't flicker. "I've seen him already today," he replied shortly. "He has friends going up to see him this afternoon."

Ashley felt a twinge of irritation. Damn it, his father wasn't a murderer or a rapist, or even a lecherous old goat. So why was she being kept away from him as if her presence would affect him with the plague? It didn't make sense. But then there were a lot of things about Gray that made no sense. She might be in love with him, but that didn't mean she was blind to the truth. Loving Gray would never be easy.

She decided to drop the subject. It was best just to enjoy being with him.

They had lunch at Thunder Bay's best hotel, and Ashley would have been self-conscious in her sweater and pants if Gray hadn't been with her. But he too was dressed casually, and in spite of that they were shown to the best and most secluded table. She had a feeling that, even if Gray hadn't been who he was, his presence would still have commanded—and got—immediate attention.

After a leisurely meal during which they discussed the food, the weather and Ashley's views on economics—which caused Gray to raise his eyebrows—they drove to the hospital to visit Nick, who was delighted to see them. He said his parents were coming soon, and it was a good thing Gray had arrived first when no one was around to fuss about boring things like medicine and resting.

Ashley grinned. Her young brother was obviously well on the road to coming home in plenty of time to disrupt the household for Christmas.

They left when Toivo and Rosa arrived, but only after Nick had extracted Gray's promise to return as soon as he could.

"He doesn't care a bit whether I show up again or not," laughed Ashley when they reached the lobby.

"A very discriminating young man," acknowledged Gray with a grin. Before she could reply, he added quickly, "I've just remembered something. Wait here, I'll be down in a minute."

Ashley blinked, as he shot back into the elevator just as the doors were closing. She knew without being told that he'd gone to have a word with his father. She frowned, and slumped down onto the nearest orange waiting room chair.

Gray wasn't gone long, but when he stepped off the elevator Ashley saw at once that something had disturbed him. His lips were grimly set, and there was a look in his eyes that boded ill for her hopes of a happy and relaxed afternoon.

"How was he?" she inquired dryly, seeing no reason to pander to his moods.

He gave her a look that left her even more convinced that this afternoon was going to prove difficult.

"Couldn't resist it, could you?" he taunted.

"Resist what?"

"Letting me know you knew where I'd been."

Ashley, who was walking across the hall to meet him, stopped dead in her tracks. "Is there any reason I shouldn't let you know?" she asked levelly. "I get the distinct impression you've been reading too many spy novels lately, McGraw. This cloak-and-dagger stuff isn't in the least bit amusing."

"It isn't meant to be," he replied, sounding bored. "And if you must know, I never read spy novels."

"Then why are you so damned secretive?"

"I didn't realize I was." He took her arm and hurried her to the door, where they nearly collided with a small woman hidden behind what appeared to be a traveling garden.

Ashley evaded the flowers and stared up at Gray in disbelief. "Gray McGraw," she said, after a moment of astonished silence, "how can you possibly say that and still manage to keep a straight face?"

Gray muttered something she didn't catch.

"And you can stop growling, or I'm going home," she told him flatly.

"No, you're not."

As she opened her mouth to tell him she'd do exactly as she pleased, he put a hand firmly on her shoulder and said mildly but with an undertone of iron, "If you were planning to indulge in a fit of indignation you should have come dressed for it, shouldn't you? In case you hadn't noticed, it snowed last night, and, although those boots you're wearing are very elegant, they definitely weren't built for serious walking."

She glanced down at the footwear in question. He was right, it had only been a light snowfall, but she would find it heavy going if she had to plough through the streets dressed like this. And of course there wasn't a hope in hell that Gray would behave like a gentleman and drive her home.

"All right," she said flatly. "*I* won't go home, *you'll* keep on growling and being secretive, and the two of us will have a charming afternoon dreaming up suitably unpleasant fates for each other. Boiling oil in your case, I think."

To her surprise, instead of snapping back at her, Gray laughed.

"Listen, Ashley," he said as their breath misted in the wintry air, "there are some things I'd rather not discuss. You'll have to accept that."

Ashley wasn't sure she had to accept anything, but, if she wanted to spend any time with Gray, she supposed she hadn't much choice. Mystery seemed to go with the territory.

"Okay," she said reluctantly, as his gaze pinned her with a steely softness. "But I *don't* have to accept any more growling."

"It's a deal." His smile was firm and sensuous. "I promise not to growl if you promise not to ask questions."

Ashley nodded, knowing it was the best she could hope for if they weren't to have a very fraught afternoon.

A short time later Gray stopped the car at the edge of a flooded playing field that had frozen into a shining sheet of ice from which all traces of last night's snow had disappeared. About a dozen youthful figures were skating on it with happy disregard for the cold.

When Ashley, in sudden consternation, remembered that she hadn't brought her skates, Gray produced a pair from the back seat.

"I really shouldn't be wearing these, you know," she protested a few minutes later, as he placed a possessive arm around her waist to lead her out on to the ice.

"Wearing what?" he inquired.

"These skates, of course. They belong to the shop."

"Oh. You had my hopes up for a moment there." His fingers touched the waistband of her pants.

Ashley glared at him.

"Sorry. And the skates are yours."

She glanced at his face and came to the immediate conclusion that he wasn't sorry at all. "But I can't accept——"

"Stop arguing with me, for heaven's sake!"

"Are you going to start growling again?" she demanded.

"Very definitely, if you don't stop arguing. Come here."

He pulled her so close that her pulse began to speed up at once, and in a moment they were on the ice in the midst of a laughing throng of children. Even through the thickness of their clothing, and with the air cold and bracing on her skin, Ashley was conscious of strength in the arm placed so proprietorially on her waist, and of power in the athletic body guiding her expertly through the shouting boys and girls.

"We're the oldest kids here," she observed, as a small boy in a blue hat narrowly missed her for the third time in under two minutes.

"I know. This is where I used to skate as a boy."

"You mean for fun?"

"Why else?" he queried.

"I don't know. I thought skating was always serious business with you."

"It was later on. Not at first." His tone was abrupt, and Ashley, who was getting quite good at reading his moods, recognized at once that the conversation had once again strayed on to dangerous ground.

She was searching for a quick change of topic when the boy in the blue hat came up and asked for Gray's autograph. Soon they were surrounded by eager children waving grubby pieces of paper to be signed, and Gray obliged each one of them with a smile, a personal comment, and a friendly word. Ashley had to bite her tongue to stop herself from remarking that it would be nice if he could be equally patient with adults.

They didn't stay long once their cover was blown, because by then the chilly sun was going down, and Gray suggested that it was time they made their way home.

"Whose home?" she asked, hoping her sudden nervousness didn't show.

"Mine, of course. Mrs. Green has left another creation in the oven, and Daisy hasn't been fed."

Ashley nodded and said she supposed that was all right, then, although in truth she had a feeling that, if she followed her inclinations, it might turn out to be all wrong.

Daisy greeted them ecstatically, her shaggy snowshoe feet landing heavily on Ashley's shoulders.

"She approves of you," said Gray as he ordered her down. "That animated carpet has more taste than I gave her credit for."

Ashley felt an absurd glow of warmth.

Later, after another mouthwatering meal—this time consumed without argument from Ashley—Gray lit a fire in the green mosaic fireplace that dominated one wall of the living room, and led her to a low white sofa facing a plate-glass window. It stretched from the floor almost to the ceiling, and seemed at odds with the house's strictly Victorian facade. She remembered that Gray had told her he liked space.

"Why did you turn the light off?" she asked, her voice rather higher than usual.

"Why not?" He sat down beside her, but didn't touch her. "Don't you like the view?"

With the jade green curtains drawn back, the big window looked out on an expanse of clean, crystalline snow unspoiled by tire marks or people. At the bottom of the garden three tall pines stood sentinel against the night, lit by a pale glow from distant lights that reflected the fine frosting of snow along the branches. It was a peaceful scene, quiet. And it made her feel strangely secure.

"Yes," she replied, "I love it. It's beautiful."

He took her hand. "So you see we don't really need the light."

But just as he spoke, almost as if some celestial hand had pulled a switch, the darkness came alive with light. Bright, glittering shards that dropped like darts into the night sky, expanding into billowing mistlike folds that moved and changed across the heavens in sheets of shimmering shot silk, reflecting the colors of winter. Blue, pale green and soft white—rippling, turning, touching the world with the gentle magic of dreams.

"Oh," breathed Ashley. "The Northern Lights!"

"Aurora Borealis," said Gray.

Then they were both silent, spellbound by a vision of the heavens that to Ashley seemed almost like an omen. Whether the omen was bad or good she wasn't sure.

But she knew now what she wanted.

After a while Gray asked softly, "Did you know that a long time ago after the great flood, the whole world was dark? And the Great Manitou covered the northern polar cap with ice crystals as high as mountains to capture the rays of the sun, so he could guide the forefathers of our native people to this land? And the ice prisms split the sun's rays into all the colors of the spectrum." He slid his arm around her shoulder. "That's why, for thousands of years now, when it's very cold, people have always been able to see the Northern Lights."

Ashley turned her head to look up at him, but his face was only a shadowed outline. The lights were fading now, becoming pale and transparent. Soon they would be gone.

"I thought," she said, a little breathlessly because she was confused by this unexpectedly whimsical Gray, and wasn't sure how to respond, "that the Lights occur when solar flares send out streams of subatomic particles which are trapped by the earth's magnetic field, and then interact with molecules in the upper atmosphere..."

Gray groaned. "There's no poetry in your soul, Ashley," he said reproachfully.

"Well, not much," she agreed, resting her head on his shoulder and feeling surprisingly safe and at peace. "It's difficult to feel poetic when Gina's screaming, Dad's playing Wagner, Sophia's rattling the bathroom door and Mom's shouting at them all to shut up."

Gray laughed. "Poor Ashley," he murmured. "We'll have to do something about that, won't we?"

"About what?"

"Your depressingly prosaic attitude to life. My life has hardly been poetic either, as far as that goes, but it's not good for the soul to be as practical as you are."

"I always thought *you* were practical," said Ashley, a trifle huffily. He might be teasing her, but she had a feeling he was criticizing as well.

"Oh, I am—when the time's appropriate." She was sure his eyes were mocking her even though she couldn't see them.

"I liked your legend, though," she admitted grudgingly.

"Did you? Then perhaps there's hope for you yet." Abruptly he withdrew his arm and pulled her around to face him. Now she could just make out his eyes, and the shape of his mouth which was advancing toward her with heart-stopping purpose. Suddenly she was uncomfortably conscious that she was alone in the house with only a sleeping dog between her and this dangerously fascinating man.

"Is the time appropriate now?" she gasped inanely.

"What?" His mouth stopped advancing. "What are you talking about, Ashley?"

"You said—you said you were practical when the time was right. Are you being—practical now?"

"I suppose I am," he replied, putting a hand on the back of her head and ruffling her hair. "It's a beautiful, romantic night, you're not mad at me for a change——"

"And you think you might as well take advantage of the opportunity," said Ashley bleakly.

His fingers in her hair stilled at once. "No. But I was planning on biding my time, and hoping that eventually you would—want me as much as I want you."

"In other words, you're hoping to seduce me."

"Is there something wrong with that? Yes, I'd like to take you to bed." His hand curved deliberately around her neck, massaging it gently and sending warm shivers down her spine.

"Why?" she whispered, utterly devastated by his touch, but too hypnotized to move away. "Why, Gray?"

He laughed, a short, explosive sort of laugh. "Why? For the Lord's sake, Ashley..." He ran his free hand quickly through his hair and then said flatly, "All the usual reasons, I suppose."

"That's what I thought," she said dully, watching the firelight flicker on his face. It made him look dark, shadowy, mysterious and a little frightening—and yet so warmly desirable that she wanted to reach out, pull his head against her breast, run her hands over his hard body and do all those things that she had once assured him she just didn't do.

And if, by some miracle, he had said he loved her, there wouldn't have been any more to be said.

She knew that now. The reason she had never been remotely tempted to give in to any of those other young men who had tried their luck was that she hadn't loved them. It was that simple. Her determination to find a home and a peace of her own had been a smoke screen behind which she had hidden her real needs from herself. And what she needed now, needed and wanted desperately and without much hope, was Gray as a permanent part of her life. That had become clear to her in one breathtaking moment, just as the Northern Lights lit the sky. But the lights had faded now, returned perhaps to Gray's crystals as high as frozen mountains.

"And there's not a chance," she murmured, not realizing she was speaking out loud.

"Isn't there?" said Gray, not unnaturally assuming she meant something quite different. "Are you sure of that, Ashley? I read somewhere that chastity is curable if detected early."

Ashley choked. "You read too much," she muttered. "It doesn't go with your image."

"I don't see why not," he replied. "Just because I have, on occasions, flattened an opponent with my fists, it doesn't mean there's no life above my neck."

"Um—no, of course not," she agreed, flustered because for the last few minutes her mind had been concentrated disturbingly on the life below his waist. "I— er..."

He put both arms around her and pulled her to him, and when he slid his firm hands slowly down her thighs, she gave up trying to think at all.

A log caught in the fireplace, sending a bright flare of orange across the ceiling. As Gray's lips closed over hers and he pushed her back against the cushions, she gasped, and gave up fighting the inevitable. She couldn't fight any more, couldn't resist him. Didn't *want* to resist him.

She gave a little cry as he turned her on her side, lifted her legs from the floor and stretched his own lean length beside her. She could feel his hands moving tantalizingly beneath her sweater and, hardly aware of what she was doing, she began to fumble with the buttons at his neck.

"Ashley," he murmured against her throat. "Ashley, my beautiful, gentle, sweet Ashley..."

The fire sparked and cracked loudly, and Daisy, who had been lying in front of it, growled softly in her sleep.

Her growl, rumbling across the dark room, roused Ashley from her own dream world, reminding her at once that the man who was lying half on top of her with his hand warm and firm on her stomach was the same man who sometimes growled at her in a manner not altogether unlike Daisy's. The man who wanted to seduce her for "all the usual reasons."

"Gray," she gasped, pressing her palms against his chest. "Gray, no..."

She felt him tense, heard him draw in his breath. "What is it?" he asked—and she knew it was costing him every ounce of the considerable control he possessed not to ignore her protest and carry on with the business that had been his aim from almost the first moment they had met. He had never made a secret of that.

She searched for words to tell him why she couldn't give him what he wanted. Words that wouldn't betray that she loved him, couldn't bear the thought of giving herself to a man who didn't love her. To her mind love was a two-way street, and, although she knew now that what she felt for Gray, with such painful intensity, was not just for today, but for forever, she also knew he had no such feelings for her. To him she was just Sweet Ashley, who might do him very nicely in bed.

"I—I just can't, Gray," she whispered, as his hand began to move again, gently caressing her hip. "Please..."

He stopped at once, pulled her sweater roughly around her waist, and sat up. "Still too soon, is it?" he said, his voice gruff and hard-edged.

Ashley stared dumbly at his back as he propped his elbows on his knees and rested his forehead on his hands.

"I—yes," she murmured. "Yes, it is. I'm sorry..."

"No reason why you should be." He dropped his arms to his knees and turned to face her, his lips curving crookedly as he took a long, very deep breath. "Don't worry, my dear. Although you probably don't believe it, I can be a remarkably patient man."

"Can you?" said Ashley, wondering why her words sounded hoarse. "But, Gray, I already told you, it's—that's just not something I do."

"There's always a first time."

Not for her there wouldn't be, she reflected sadly. She had, briefly, thought about having the affair he wanted. But now she knew she couldn't do it.

So there wouldn't be a first time. Not ever. Not for her. She heard a choked sob catch in her throat.

"Hey," said Gray, hearing it too, "what's this? Ashley, I said I'd wait—not that I intended to rape you."

"I know," Ashley sniffed. "It's all right, I'm not crying."

"Then what's the matter?" His tone was tinged with impatience, and she couldn't blame him.

"Nothing."

"Oh, I see." Abruptly Gray rose to his feet and strode across the room to switch the light on. His eyes, when he turned to face her, were very dark. "I see. Your pretty mouth is quivering like unset jelly, your lovely eyes resemble twin puddles that are about to turn into pools, and if I'm not mistaken, that's a tributary running down your cheek. Yet you tell me there's nothing the matter."

"There isn't. And I'm not jelly." She sniffed again, and groped in her pocket for a handkerchief, which proved futile because there weren't any pockets in her pants.

"Oh, for heaven's sake," muttered Gray. "Here." He crossed the room, sat down beside her, and handed her a white linen square. When she began to dab ineffectually at her face, he took it back from her and did the job himself.

"There," he said, when her skin was dry and shiny again, and she sat looking at him with eyes that were still enormous, but no longer like overflowing pools, "that's better. Now what's this all about, Ashley? I'm not going to hurt you, I'm not going to make you do anything you don't want to do, and, if you insist, I'll even take you home without making the slightest attempt to remove anything you want to keep on—which as far as I'm concerned will be a waste of a promising evening."

"Is that all you brought me here for?" asked Ashley in a small voice.

His eyebrows rose in a cynical arc, which made him look more like a pirate than ever. "All?" he repeated. "Is the prospect of making love to me such a bore, then?"

He knew it wasn't. She could tell from the sensuous slant of his mouth.

"No," she said, "it's not, as you very well know." Inadvertently her eyes dropped to his waist, and she saw the wide leather belt molding his hips and the taut curve of his thighs in tight denim. She swallowed, and when she looked up again she noted that his lips were more predatory than before, and his eyes very bright and intent.

She started over. "It wouldn't be a bore. And I—I like being with you, Gray." Surely it was safe to admit that much. "But I'm not going to bed with you. And if that's all you want, we might as well end our—our friendship, right now."

"Mmm." Gray eyed her reflectively, his expression hard to interpret. "We might. But we're not going to. I like being with you too—contrary and disobliging as you are."

"Disobliging?" echoed Ashley. "Is it disobliging to refuse——?"

"Very," said Gray. But he was grinning now, and she knew the dangerous moment had passed.

A little tentatively, she grinned back.

"Yes, that's much better," he approved. "Some women may look beautiful when they cry, but you're not one of them."

"Thanks," said Ashley, not in the least offended. This mocking, unflattering Gray she could cope with. "And I suppose *you* never cry, and consequently remain a permanently handsome hazard to the female sex."

His grin broadened into a leer, although when he spoke there was an unexpected bleakness in his tone. "Any man with the ability to feel has shed tears, Ashley. But no, I don't make a habit of it. And I'm delighted to know you consider me a handsome hazard. In fact it encourages me to think this evening needn't be wasted after all."

"Gray..." she said warningly, edging away from him and coming up against the arm of the sofa. "Gray, no..."

"It's all right, little rabbit." His voice was very soft now, and his hands settled on her waist with determination. "Don't be frightened, I'm only going to kiss you."

"I'm not frightened. And you mustn't kiss me, because——"

Then she couldn't remember why he mustn't kiss her, because he was. Expertly, lingeringly, his hands moving from her waist to her back to hold her close. So close that she could hardly breathe. And somehow she was lying against the cushions again with his tough body stretched across her. She gave a little murmur and pushed her fingers into the springy strength of his hair, kissing him back and holding his mouth hard on hers.

When his hand slipped down to stroke her thigh with a slow, erotic motion, she gave a soft groan and reached for his belt. She felt the taut male skin beneath her fingers, and in that moment, to her utter confusion, Gray pushed her arm away and sat up.

She stared at him, breathing very fast, and saw that he was breathing hard too. His eyes were darker than ever now, deep and seductive as velvet.

"Ashley?" His voice was husky, demanding, and she couldn't fail to understand the question.

"I——" She moistened her lips, hypnotized like the rabbit he had called her. And she wanted him more desperately than before. Perhaps—perhaps... No. This time, if he hadn't stopped, she would have given in—to herself as well as to him. But that would have been wrong. He didn't love her, only liked her a little and probably enjoyed the challenge she presented. Once he was satisfied, had what he wanted, she would become just another of the conquests he had managed to make time for. She couldn't live with that—she couldn't. It would break her heart.

"No," she said, moving her head against the cushion. "No, Gray—I'm sorry. It wouldn't be right."

He sighed and stood up abruptly, ramming his hands into the pockets of his jeans as he stared down at her with a twisted smile pulling at his lips. He looked achingly desirable, thought Ashley, with his dark hair all disheveled, his black shirt open to the waist and his legs apart as if he could straddle the world if he chose to.

"Still the little puritan," he said, shaking his head. "Soon we'll have to do something to change that. But not yet." He spoke softly, and he was still smiling, but the words sent a chill up Ashley's spine. Not because she was afraid of him particularly, but because she was afraid of herself.

"No," she said again, sitting up, and pushing uselessly at her hair. "No, Gray, we're not going to change it. And I think it's better if we don't see each other any more."

"That speech is becoming quite tedious," he told her flatly. "And I don't want to hear it again."

"But..."

"Don't give me buts, Ashley. I intend to see more of you, and that's that. You've told me you like being with me, so that's a start. It'll be Christmas in a few weeks." His lip curled in a grimace that was half mockery, half pure seduction. "Perhaps you'll decide to give me the present I want."

Ashley stared at him, standing there tall and sexy, and completely confident of his power to get what he wanted. And she felt as if a great stone had settled on her chest, a stone that would be there forever.

"I'll take you home now," he went on, as if nothing had happened between them, "and I'll pick you up on Wednesday after your exam."

Ashley knew she ought to tell him he wouldn't do anything of the sort. But she didn't, because she couldn't bear the thought that she might not see him again.

When Wednesday came, he picked her up as planned.

On Friday he was there when she left Mr. White's, but he didn't have to kidnap her this time. After several restless nights and a great many despairing discussions with Maria, Ashley had come to the conclusion that she might as well enjoy Gray's company while she could. A few days or a few weeks would be little enough to remember in the long, lonely years that stretched ahead.

Maria was disgusted with her sister for not striking while the iron was hot, the iron in this case being Gray, whose heat was fairly evident to anyone who took time to notice the way he looked at Ashley. Maria had taken time when he brought Ashley home on Friday night. She also told her sister that Gray had been into the shop on several occasions, and was getting very short-tempered.

"He's always short-tempered," Ashley replied dismissively.

It wasn't entirely true, though, because in the weeks leading up to Christmas he was very considerate, understanding that she had to study for exams and ready to take her out when she had the time. She guessed that his father was home from the hospital now, though, because he didn't take her to his house any more. Instead they went cross-country skiing, or skating when the sun was shining, and to dinner in places which Ashley's previous escorts had never been able to afford. Quite often Rosa persuaded Gray to stay with the family for supper. All of them now regarded him as one of themselves, and made no effort to tone down the noise level for his benefit.

When, just two days before Christmas, Nick came home, unbandaged and proudly exhibiting his scars, the jubilation rose to such ear-splitting heights that, after one look at Ashley's strained face, Gray promised to take her out for a quiet meal alone on Christmas Eve.

She agreed out of sheer desperation, although she was afraid that dinner would precede another quietly determined attempt to convince her that physical abstinence was unhealthy, unnecessary, and prudish. Not that he had been at all pressing in that regard lately. In fact he had been the soul of restraint, contenting himself with light kisses, and treating her with quiet possessiveness and a teasing, gentle derision. All the same, Ashley didn't believe that would last, and sometimes she almost wished it wouldn't, because this arm's length contact was beginning to drive her crazy. If only, she thought wearily, she didn't love him so much. But she did, and even though she had to keep reminding herself there was no future in it, loving him, she wanted to make him happy.

Once, tentatively, she had broached the subject of his father, but he had responded with an almost savage command to "drop it." That could only mean he didn't think of her as permanent. She was not to become privy to his private burdens. In other words, she was just another ship that would pass in the night. And in the end she would be left to sail on alone.

Perhaps fortunately, such wistful musings were impossible to maintain on Christmas Eve. Pandemonium reigned in the Kalani house as usual, exacerbated by excitement and the prospect of presents to be opened at midnight, according to the family tradition. Ashley was glad that the festive food was not be be consumed until Christmas Day and that the early part of the evening was hers to do with as she pleased. She was also so thankful to be escaping the chaos for a few hours that when she heard Gray's loud knock on the door she rushed to open it, tripping over the telephone table and greeting him with an ecstatic and spontaneous hug that surprised her as much as it did him.

"Well, well, well, things *are* looking up!" he murmured, his eyes running approvingly over the soft curves of her body, which were more evident than usual this evening, accentuated by the folds of her revealing red "special occasion" dress.

Behind them, Sophia and Maria burst into delighted applause. Nick, who was by no means as immobile as he was meant to be, gave a disgusted groan and muttered, "Oh, yuck, Gray! You're not going to get all slobbery over Ashley, are you?"

"I sincerely hope not," said Gray, his lips quirking. "I usually leave that sort of thing to Daisy."

To Ashley's enormous relief, for once Gray seemed as anxious to get away as she was, and a short time later they were sitting down to a quiet drink in the dining room of one of the city's better hotels. As the peace and restrained luxury closed around them, she heaved a sigh of pure, unadulterated gratitude.

"Thank you," she said, with heartfelt sincerity. "I do love my family, Gray, really I do, but sometimes, especially around Christmas, I just need——"

"Space?" he suggested, smiling.

"Yes, that's it exactly. How did you know?"

His eyes laughed at her. "I'm not sure, but over these last few weeks I think I've come to know you rather well."

"Have you?" said Ashley, blinking. His discerning gaze made her self-conscious.

"Mmm, I think so."

"What else do you know about me?" she asked, wondering if the question would prove wise.

"Oh..." he shut his eyes, and pretended to think about it "...that you're funny and honest and loyal, that you like dogs and don't like noise, that you're a practical young lady at heart..." His eyes snapped open abruptly, piercing her with their sudden intensity. "And that you're a warm and very desirable young woman who's too damned obstinate for her own good."

"For *your* own good, you mean," she corrected him, feeling as if she'd just been slapped in the face.

"No," he shook his head and raised his glass very deliberately, "not only mine. Here's to us, Ashley. To the New Year and—new experiences."

She lifted her glass. "To Christmas and the New Year," she said cautiously.

"Ah, yes, Christmas." Now he was regarding her with a penetration that sent familiar shivers down her spine. "Have I been patient enough for you, Ashley? Am I going to get the present I want?"

She'd known it was too good to last. He'd been so undemanding lately, quite different from the tough, aggressive man she'd worked for in those early weeks at Boyko's. But she had felt all along that he was holding something in by the sheer force of his considerable willpower. And now it was out in the open. The old, demanding Gray was back, expecting to get what he wanted and determined to have it. That glitter in his eyes was devastatingly sensual, making her want to climb across the table into his arms. It was also quite ruthlessly businesslike. As if he'd waited as long as was reasonable, and intended to start serious negotiations at once.

But she wasn't a deal to be worked out.

"No," she said, her fingers clamping so tightly around her glass that Gray was obliged to remove it. "No. I do have a present for you, but I'm afraid it's not what you want."

"I see," he said, to her astonishment sounding almost indifferent. "I suppose I should have expected that. My timing was off, wasn't it? But you seemed—different tonight. I hoped..."

"You hoped I'd be more—accommodating," said Ashley, her voice cracking.

Gray glanced at her sharply. "I suppose I did. Why aren't you—accommodating, Ashley?"

She swallowed, tears very close to the surface, and unaware that her eyes reflected such anguish that for a moment Gray's face went tight with shock.

"I can't be," she whispered. "I can't say yes to you, Gray. It—it would hurt too much."

CHAPTER NINE

THE knuckles on Gray's closed fist shone palely beneath the light, and when Ashley raised her eyes she saw deep grooves carved beside his mouth. His nostrils were flared as if he'd had an unwanted and devastating revelation. But she didn't think he was angry, just appalled and deeply disturbed.

"Ashley," he said, his voice echoing some emotion she didn't recognize, "Ashley, I know you don't have a high opinion of my former life-style, but I do have *some* sense of decency. Can't you please get it fixed in your brain that I'm not a monster? I wouldn't get any kick out of hurting you—or anyone else."

Ashley shook her head. "I didn't mean that kind of hurt," she said, staring at the clean white tablecloth and wishing she were a thousand miles away—in a coma— where nothing and nobody, especially Gray, could possibly hurt her. "I meant—I meant..." She glanced at him doubtfully and saw that his eyes had narrowed. "I meant—it would hurt—in other ways..."

She *couldn't* tell him she loved him, and that the pain would be emotional, not physical. Not when he was staring at her with that grim, reflective concentration that she couldn't even begin to understand.

"Other ways?" said Gray. He closed his eyes. "Yes, I think I see."

"Do you?" she asked, almost sure he didn't.

He gave no answer, because the waiter arrived then to take their order, and, when he left, they relapsed into silence.

151

It was a very strained meal that followed, with both of them disinclined to speak—until about halfway through the dessert, when Gray remarked, with what Ashley assumed was an attempt to make conversation, that, if there were many more women like her, heaven's stock of haloes would soon run out.

She smiled thinly, said, "Pinero. Don't plagiarize," and went doggedly on with her charlotte russe. Gray's knowledge of books and playwrights had long since ceased to surprise her, but at the moment she was in no mood to endure literary banter about her alleged virtue. Especially as she suspected he meant it.

Was it just the fact that he wasn't getting his own way that rankled? she wondered as she put down her spoon. Or was it something else? Surely there was more than just wounded ego behind the way she had caught him looking at her when he thought she was absorbed with her trout. It was almost as if he was trying to make a decision that was supposed to be about business, but had turned into something agonizingly personal instead. And it was apparent that he didn't like the direction his thoughts were taking. He didn't seem to be liking anything much at the moment, she noted glumly, as she watched him push his plate away with half his meal still untouched.

A minute later she knew that whatever he was trying to make up his mind about had been decided, because his face became curiously set, and he leaned back in his chair and said curtly, "I'd better get you home, if you've finished. Your family will be expecting you, I imagine?"

"Yes—soon." Ashley felt the first stirrings of indignation. She didn't want to tell him that she wouldn't be expected for another hour. Not when he was so patently anxious to be rid of her. But nor did she appreciate being treated like excess baggage.

"I'm not baggage," she muttered.

Gray's eyebrows lifted a fraction. "Hmm, debatable," he murmured, and went off to get their coats.

Ashley glowered at his departing back and wished she didn't find it so attractive.

To her surprise, when they arrived at the bottom of her street after an uncomfortably silent drive home, he stopped the car abruptly instead of pulling up in front of her house. She decided he probably wanted to avoid the prying eyes of her sisters, and felt a quick surge of alarm—followed by a growing anticipation.

But, to her relief as well as her disappointment, Gray made no attempt to touch her. Instead he rested his hand on top of the wheel, turned to face her and said, unusually quietly for him, "This has to be goodbye, Ashley. I'm sorry."

She knew at once that he didn't mean just for this evening, and she made a small sound that was partly indignation and partly a cry of pain.

He heard her, and turned away. "I said I don't want to hurt you, and I meant it." The words were flat, spoken without emotion, and Ashley wondered if she was only imagining the depth of feeling she sensed behind them.

"I..." She didn't know what to say. This was all wrong. *She* was the one who was supposed to break it off—as she had tried to do several times already. But this time he was agreeing with her, and, if she hadn't known it before, she knew now, with a crushing dismay, that she hadn't meant a word of it when she'd suggested it was time to end their tenuous friendship.

"Why?" she eventually managed to croak. "Because I won't sleep with you?"

No. That sounded as if she were protesting, and she was damned if she would let him know how much she cared. She took a deep breath, and said in a firmer tone, "Not that it matters, because of course you're right—

this should never have started. As I believe I tried to point out to you before."

"Yes, you did. I'm sorry, Ashley, I should have known better." His knuckles tightened on the wheel. "You ask why, and I can't answer you. But please believe me. It's over."

She stared at his face as he turned back to her in the pale glare of the street light. It was closed, hard as granite, wiped clean of emotion. Not as if he cared at all. As though he had suddenly become bored with her and wanted to get this tiresome scene over with as quickly and as easily as he could. Except—was there something? Something he wanted to say, but was determined should remain unspoken? She dropped her eyes to the expertly knotted tie at his neck. If he wanted to keep his own counsel, who was she to change his mind? The woman who loved him, that was who, she answered herself. Only that didn't seem to matter to him at all. If he guessed— which she hoped he didn't.

"I dare say I'll survive," she said, putting every ounce of courage she'd ever possessed into the effort to sound casually unconcerned. "Nothing vital has been lost. It doesn't matter."

But it did matter, and something very vital had been lost. It was called her heart.

He lowered his eyelids, so that all she could see was the dark arch of his heavy brows. "Good." His response was brisk, unbearably businesslike. "Thank you, Ashley. I don't like scenes."

Oh, he didn't like scenes! As if she'd have given him the satisfaction of making one. Dammit, *he* was the one who had initiated this whole disaster. And now he was coolly telling her it was over. Because it no longer suited him to waste his time on the last of the dedicated virgins, she supposed.

"I don't care for scenes either," she told him, refusing to let her hurt show. "Frankly, it'll be quite a relief to be able to get on with my studies without you hanging around to waste my time."

"Oh, will it?" He no longer sounded quite so uninterested. "In that case, I'll leave you with something to think about while you're enjoying all that newfound freedom."

He reached for her, and Ashley started back against the door.

"Don't worry," he drawled softly, "I'm not about to help myself to your most prized possession."

As she pressed against the door, her eyes wide, and her fingers groping behind her for the handle, he eased himself across the seat and helped himself, not to her most prized possession, but to her lips.

His kiss was hard, almost savage, and his hands explored the rest of her with a practiced thoroughness that sent the blood roiling in her veins. It seemed to go on for a long time. She sat quite still, driven by a desperate longing to respond, and yet numbed by the unfeeling skill with which he seemed to be manipulating her senses. Was he deliberately trying to hurt her? He didn't really seem involved in what he was doing at all. She was being kissed by a robot...

Who was turning into the man she loved.

His kiss became gentler, more truly passionate, and the hands that had been moving roughly over her body gentled too. He lifted his mouth from hers and held her head against his chest.

"Merry Christmas, Ashley," he said gruffly. "And thank you—for everything." He let her go.

Blindly Ashley reached for the door.

"No, wait, I'll drive you to your house," he said quickly.

"It's only half a block." She couldn't look at him. "I can use the exercise."

"Don't be a..."

But she wasn't listening. Her fingers found the handle, and she stumbled out into the snow.

"Ashley, wait..."

Gray grabbed her arm as she moved away. He was leaning out of the car, and his free hand held a small, wrapped package. "Here," he said, handing it to her with a look in his eyes that, just for a moment, made her heart sing with hope. "This is for you."

"No." She shook her head as hope faded into reality. "Please let me go."

"Take it—I want you to have it."

She started to refuse again, but he was still holding her arm, and suddenly she couldn't bear it any more. As usual, what Gray wanted, he got. She took the package without looking at it and shoved it into her pocket. Her fingers encountered something hard.

"Oh," she whispered, pulling out a small box and still not looking at him. "Here, you might as well have this too."

Then she turned on her heel and hurried away along the frozen pavement.

She was already at her gate by the time he had gunned his engine and caught up with her, but, although she knew he would watch until she was safely in the house, she kept her eyes firmly fixed on the door.

The celebrations inside were already reaching a crescendo, so she didn't hear Gray's car pull away.

But she knew it had.

"Hey, Ash..." Rocky erupted into the hall like a Christmas missile, trailing several rolls of green paper and a large ball of blue glitter twine. "Ash, do you know what happened to that box of stickers? I'm trying to wrap Mom's present, and——"

"Yes," interrupted Ashley tiredly. "Carlo and Nick used them all on that model space station they made for Dad."

"Damn," said Rocky. "Rotten little reptiles! Can't they ever think of the rest of us?"

Ashley was of the opinion that no one in this house thought much of anyone else unless it suited them. Except her parents, of course, and sometimes Maria. But she didn't say so. She didn't even bother to tell Rocky that that was no way to speak of his brothers. Instead she stamped up the stairs to her room and shut the door.

It didn't help much. The sound of Rocky yelling at Nick and Carlo carried easily up through the floor. So did a loud burst of tuneless caroling inflicted on her long-suffering family by Gina.

Ashley glanced at her watch. Still an hour to go until midnight. She couldn't even go to bed, although all she wanted to do was curl up into a little ball and die. Preferably after she'd administered a large dose of arsenic to the Great McGraw, who had just added another victim to his impressive list. She could have saved herself a lot of grief if she'd paid attention to all that gossip in the papers...

She sat down heavily on the edge of the bed and stared at the disapproving face of Aunt Dorinda. She wondered if she would look like that when she was eighty—dried up and grim and bitter.

Gray was gone. He might be a world-class rat, whom she was much better off without. But mostly he was just—gone. The word kept pounding in her head.

The worst part of it was that she wasn't even sure what had happened. It looked as though Gray had picked to-night for the big seduction, while she was supposed to be all softened up and tender with Christmas spirit. Although how he'd thought seduction could be fitted in neatly between dinner and midnight she couldn't think.

In any case, she had nipped his little scheme in the bud, and right after that he had decided to call the whole thing off.

She scowled and squeezed her eyes shut, knowing that crying could accomplish nothing. If only he hadn't chosen Christmas Eve...

But he couldn't be held entirely to blame, she tried to convince herself, twisting a corner of the bedspread. One had to be fair... No, like hell one did. He had just destroyed all her dreams, and fairness didn't enter into the matter. Just because she had always assured him that she had no ambitions in the white lace and orange-blossom line, it didn't mean he had the right to break her heart.

Only perhaps he really hadn't understood that his leaving her would be the end of everything that mattered. It had taken her long enough to find that out herself.

Biting her lip, she stood up to remove her coat, along with the bright red dress, and as she peeled it off she caught a glimpse of its fiery allure in the mirror.

How Gray's eyes had glinted when he had seen her in it.

She paused with the dress halfway over her head. What if he had assumed it was in the nature of an invitation? And what if—what if she were to change her mind? Phone him and tell him he could have the present he wanted...

Great-Aunt Dorinda glared balefully. Ashley stood for a long time glaring back.

Some time later, as the sound of Gina murdering *Good King Wenceslas* shrieked its way up from below, she groaned out loud to the picture, "You're right, Aunt D—I can't do it. I told Gray the truth when I said it would hurt too much."

"Talking to yourself, Ash?" The door crashed open, and Maria burst in, all bright-eyed, and looking thoroughly kissed. "Guess what? I went over to Jenny's, and I met this hunky new guy..." Her voice trailed off as her eyes came to rest on Ashley's streaked and stricken face. "My God! What is it, Ash? What's happened...?"

Ashley told her.

"But it's all right," she finished, rallying. "I don't need him, any more than he needs me. He's just a big oversexed jerk."

"Garbage," said Maria forthrightly. "He's nice really. And he's a hunk. Oversexed would be a bonus."

Ashley pursed her mouth and looked severe. But privately she agreed with her sister. And it didn't help.

The rest of the evening was her idea of hell. It wasn't just the noise, which she expected and understood. It was the necessity of keeping up a cheerful front, as her family unwrapped their gifts with squeals of glee—and of pretending that everything was normal, while inside her everything was raw and hurting.

The worst moment came when she discovered that Gray had left gifts for everyone. A plant for her mother, a new Wagner tape for her father, hockey sticks for the boys, and silk scarves for all the girls. Even Gina. When it became obvious that there was nothing for Ashley, it was all she could do not to burst into tears and scream at them all that there *was* something for Ashley, but she'd left it upstairs and didn't want it.

Maria understood, and sat beside her sister all evening, trying to shield her from the worst of the teasing curiosity. For that Ashley was grateful. As soon as she could, she pleaded a headache and went upstairs to her room.

Gray's package was still in her coat pocket. Listlessly, not caring much, she untied the string. The bright silver paper contained a small silver box. She opened it. Inside nestled two perfect crystal glass earrings. When she held

them up, they reflected the colors of the spectrum in a
hundred points of brilliant, stabbing light.

Ashley thought of the box she had given to Gray. She
had wanted to get him something that wasn't too grand
or ostentatious, and she had settled, in the end, on a
small, carefully cut quartz crystal that reminded her of
the shape of a mountain.

She stared at the earrings. There was no card with
them, but she knew without being told that he had been
thinking, as she had, of that evening when together they
had glimpsed a rainbow-tinted heaven. Different crystals,
symbols of the same happy memory. But, in spite of
that, tonight he had said goodbye. And somehow she
must—she *would* find the courage to get on with the life
she had planned. Without him.

Two enormous tears formed in Ashley's eyes and
meandered very slowly down her cheeks.

"Ashley Kalani?" The voice on the phone was abrupt,
like another voice she had known. Somewhere, she
thought, she'd heard it before.

"Yes," she admitted, puzzled.

"Good. Listen, this is Bruce McGraw speaking. Can
you come over to see me?"

"Now?" Ashley felt her heart thump painfully.

"Yup. My son's out."

Her pulse slowed down at once. "I—I don't know,"
she hedged, not wanting to give offense, and yet unable
to bear the thought of visiting Gray's house again.

"I need you," he insisted. "Got to talk to you. I'll
send a taxi."

"Well—yes, all right," she agreed weakly, giving in
because she didn't know what else to do. She had liked
Gray's father, and if he needed her...

Half an hour later she was seated in the back of the
taxi, trying not to hope that by some twist of fate Gray

would turn out to be there after all. Gray, who had said goodbye and meant it, because, in all the lonely weeks since they'd parted, not once had he attempted to see her. Then she remembered that Maria had told her he had been in Toronto on business for the past week.

It was the beginning of February now, and Maria still worked at Boyko's. Although she tried not to talk about her job because she knew it distressed her sister, every now and then some piece of information slipped out.

Ashley came back to her surroundings as the taxi pulled up outside the familiar three-storeyed house on High Street.

Bruce McGraw was waiting for her by the door, no longer in a wheelchair, but holding himself erect with the aid of a stick. Daisy dashed past him, nearly knocking his legs out from under him, and planted an ecstatic wet kiss on Ashley's nose.

"Damned dog," muttered Bruce with affection. "So you've managed to charm her too, girl."

Ashley smiled. "She's a charmer herself. I'm glad you're better, Mr. McGraw."

"Bruce," he corrected her. "Told you that before. And I'm not necessarily better—just happen to be on my feet."

Ashley nodded, speechless, as he stumped into the living room, after beckoning peremptorily at her to follow.

Like father, like son, she thought, feeling an all too familiar lump in her chest.

He slumped down into a large tweed armchair that didn't match the rest of the room, and waved her to the sofa she had shared with Gray. Wincing, Ashley took the seat he had indicated.

Bruce McGraw's eyes narrowed. "Hmm, been here before, haven't you?" he barked.

"Well—yes, a few times." Gray's father didn't miss much.

"Thought so. That's why I wanted to see you."

When she didn't reply, he put both hands on his knees and bent forward, studying her from under frowning bushy brows. At length he shifted his shoulders irritably and leaned back again. "You in love with my boy?" he demanded bluntly.

Ashley was horribly disconcerted to feel a blush stealing over her cheeks. "I—don't think that's any of——" she began.

"Any of my business? Course it's not. Just wanted an answer. And I think I've got it."

"Have you?" she replied faintly.

"Mmm—I think so. He's impossible to live with, you know. Growls like a bear when I speak to him, calls Daisy a misbegotten mistake every time he trips over her—and on top of that he smashed his car into the gatepost twice this past week, and only just missed a customer the other day."

"Oh, dear," said Ashley, swallowing. "That doesn't sound like Gray. I mean the growling like a bear part does, but he's usually a good driver."

"Huh, that's what I mean. He's impossible." He fixed her with what she supposed was an accusing stare. "And I'm damned sure you're the reason. He's in love with you, girl, even if he won't admit it."

Ashley gaped at him, wondering if he'd lost his mind, or if she'd lost hers.

"Did you say he's in *love* with me?" she repeated. "Because if you did, I have to tell you that what Gray feels has nothing to do with love at all."

"Rubbish—course it has! Plenty of willing women about if you happen to be rich and famous. Which he is. And he's not interested. How come all that doesn't impress *you*, Ashley Kalani?" His eyes were very bright on her face.

"I don't know," Ashley shrugged. "I guess my expectations never included fame and fortune. All I wanted was a quiet little house of my own and a good job."

"Hmm." The bright eyes narrowed, sharpened to probing black points. "No husband? No children?"

"I don't know." She wondered why she couldn't put a stop to his prying by turning it away with a laugh. "I suppose one day... I like children—some of the time, and if there aren't seven of them all screaming at once. But I haven't really thought much about having my own. I'm only twenty-two, you know, and I suppose at the moment kids aren't—well, aren't a huge priority."

"And when they are?" His voice came out in a bark.

"*If* they are, I'll cross that bridge when I come to it."

In truth, she couldn't imagine having anyone's children but Gray's, and, since that wasn't going to happen, the whole concept seemed remote, farfetched and irrelevant.

Bruce McGraw grunted. "There's hope for us, then," he remarked enigmatically.

"Hope?" Ashley was puzzled.

"Mmm." He didn't enlighten her. "Listen, girl, my boy needs you, but he's too damn stubborn to do anything about it himself. I know you've quarreled. All the same, you go to him." The eyes that had been so sharp now held a look of pleading, which she could tell he was trying to hide beneath the abrupt veneer.

"Why?" asked Ashley, with equal abruptness.

She watched the struggle reflected on Bruce's proud but still attractive face. "To please an old man," he muttered finally. His shoulders sagged. The effort of asking instead of commanding had evidently cost him a good deal.

"Yes," she said, hearing the doubt in her own voice, "I'd like to please you." She took a long breath. "I'd like to see Gray again too, but I don't think——"

"That's it—*don't* think. Just do it."

As if to add her own prompting to her master's, Daisy sat up suddenly and began to scratch, her elbow knocking noisily on the floor. Then she crossed the room and laid her muzzle in Ashley's lap, her chocolate eyes blatantly melting.

Ashley gave a shaky smile as she patted the wiry head. "All right," she agreed, giving in because it was what, in her heart, she desperately wanted to do, "I'll see him."

The morose expression Bruce had been wearing vanished at once. "Good girl," he grunted, a small smile of triumph curving his lips.

Ashley smiled too, but not with triumph. "Can I ask you something?" she inquired cautiously.

"Free country—fire away. Don't promise to answer, though."

"Well..." she wrinkled her nose "...it's just that Gray seemed so adamant that you and I shouldn't meet. It never seemed to make sense, so I wondered if you could tell me why——"

"Could. Not going to." Bruce's mouth was as obstinate as his son's when he'd made up his mind.

"Oh, I'm sorry..." Ashley was flustered, hoping she hadn't given offense.

"No need to be sorry—perfectly natural question. Can't answer it, that's all. If Gray wouldn't tell you, it means he doesn't want you to know. Also means he's a damn fool, but that's his business. If he has any sense, which I often doubt, he'll tell you himself, girl. Only chance he has, in my opinion. But it's up to him."

"Yes, of course. I see," said Ashley, who saw almost nothing in the elder McGraw's cryptic comments.

At any rate nothing that would help her.

* * *

The wind cut across the head office parking lot like an icy blade, forcing Ashley to lower her head in an effort to stave off its assault. By the time she reached the door, with the breath almost beaten from her body, her face was bright red, her hat askew and her eyes dim and watery from the cold. So much for her hopes of knocking Gray off his feet with the force of her ravishing beauty, she thought wryly.

Several times in the days following her meeting with Bruce McGraw, she had been tempted to break her unguarded promise to the old man. Gray had made it very clear that his abrupt goodbye was forever, and, if she tried to make him change his mind now, she was sure he would only rebuff her. It was agony enough living with the knowledge that she had lost him, without adding that final humiliation to her pain.

But now here she was, common sense and common self-preservation forgotten, standing in the freezing wind trying to gather up courage to make a move.

Courage had kept her going these past weeks, but this time the wind did it for her. A slice of cold air slammed against her back and down her neck, and without deliberating further, she grasped the handle and elbowed open the door.

"Mr. McGraw's out," explained the trim, gray-haired receptionist who guarded Gray's door. "He'll be back shortly. Would you care to wait?"

Ashley nodded dumbly, and was shown to a carpeted reception area decorated in luxurious black-and-gold tones. There was a brass coatrack in the corner, and she walked over to it, pulling off her gloves as she passed a white marble sculpture of an athlete throwing a ball.

Half an hour later Gray still hadn't returned, and quite suddenly Ashley knew she couldn't stay any longer. She had longed to run from the moment she had walked through the door, not wanting to face the devastating probability of Gray's rejection. But she had hung on because of her promise to Bruce McGraw—and because running was the coward's way out. Now she had waited long enough. Gray wasn't going to come, and the waiting and the memories were stifling her, had become almost more than she could bear.

"I'm getting out of here," she announced to the empty air, as she jumped to her feet and stumbled over to the coatrack. Slinging her coat over her arm, she looked vaguely around for her woolen hat and gloves. Surely she had put them beside her on the padded gold leather seat...

"Damn," she muttered, still talking to herself. "Where the hell did I put them?"

"Are you referring to your deplorably well used accessories?" inquired a caustic voice from behind her that definitely didn't belong to the receptionist. "Precisely where you left them, I imagine. Frankly, Ashley, I don't think much of your taste in corporate decoration."

CHAPTER TEN

ASHLEY, who had been peering behind the gold seat, straightened hastily, her face the color of boiled beetroot. At once she saw that the missing hat was perched jauntily on the head of the marble sculpture. The gloves were draped over its arms, turning it into something that looked more like a failed attempt to scare off birds than a work of art. She'd forgotten she had absently arranged them there when she came in.

Just inside the doorway, Gray, dressed in a dark suit and deep maroon tie, was propped against the wall with his arms crossed. The perfect model of the well-turned-out executive, thought Ashley, moving her tongue over her lips—tough, perfectly pressed, and intimidatingly powerful. His stance was deceptively casual, but she suspected that behind the carelessly arched eyebrows and the cool smile was a virile, aggressive man on the brink of a very unbusinesslike explosion.

"Hello, Gray," she said, wishing that every nerve in her body wasn't crying at her to fly into his arms—in spite of the fact that she knew she was about as welcome as a bug in one of his computer programs.

"Hello, Ashley." He continued to watch her, not moving a muscle. When she was almost ready to scream with tension, he asked brusquely, "What are you doing here?" There was nothing accommodating in his tone, nothing to make her think his father might have been right about his feelings. Certainly nothing to indicate that he loved her.

"I—I came to see you. On business," she lied, trying to salvage what was left of her pride.

"Indeed? And what kind of business would that be?"
Now he sounded more like a prosecuting attorney than
an executive. And of course he didn't believe her. Even
though his body was still draped lazily against the wall,
with his capable hands shoved deep inside his pockets,
everything about him shouted rejection. She had a feeling
that if she took a step toward him he would spin her
around and hurl her out into the gale. Which wasn't
what she had come for.

"All right," she admitted, steeling herself against the
threatened storm, "I didn't come on business. I came
to see you."

"Why?"

"Because—because . . ." Should she tell him the truth,
tell him she loved him and be damned to her idiotic
pride?

She stared at him, searching for some small sign that
behind the smoldering gaze and the flat mouth, the man
she had fallen in love with might still be there. Might
actually love her.

She didn't find it.

"Because I'm a fool," she said bitterly, pulling on her
coat while he watched her with that still, expressionless
gaze. As she headed blindly for the door she stole one
last despairing glance at his face.

"Don't forget your belongings," he said coldly. "They
don't do a thing for my décor."

Ashley turned to grab her hat and gloves off the
sculpture, pulling the planes of her face into a tight mask
so he wouldn't see that she cared.

"Don't take it too much to heart," whispered the receptionist as she hurried past. "He's just having one of
his Count Dracula days. He's had quite a few of them
lately."

Ashley couldn't take it any place but to heart as she
stumbled out into the biting wind. That was the only

part of herself she could feel at the moment, and it seemed to be breaking in two.

Later, as she sat frozen in the steamy warmth of the bus, she thought again of that look of harsh rejection on Gray's face. He had been so tightly controlled, so sternly unapproachable. It was as if she had done something unforgivable for which he was determined to punish her. Yet all she had wanted to do was offer him love.

But he hadn't offered so much as a hint of encouragement, and he had been far more hurtful than on that day when he had bade her goodbye. Then, he had at least wished her a Merry Christmas. And he had kissed her.

What had happened to turn him into the hard-faced stranger she had seen today? She thought of his eyes, so black and enigmatic in the soft glow of the office lighting. Had they really been as hard as she remembered? In those last moments, hadn't there been a kind of pain in the way his lips parted across his teeth? She could almost believe too, if she let her imagination run away with her, that there had been despair and a bleak tenderness in the way he looked at her in that instant before she turned away.

No, she must be going crazy. There had been no despair, no tenderness. Only an impatience to be rid of her. She was just something he had wanted once, a challenge he hadn't overcome, and now he had shrugged her off, moved on to the other challenges, she supposed. She stared dully at a bald patch on the head of the man in front of her, and thought of Bruce McGraw—who had been wrong, dead wrong. His son didn't love her. He didn't even care about her any more.

Surreptitiously, and angry with herself for bleeding so over a man who didn't love her and who had so recently reopened a painful wound, Ashley brushed the back of her hand across her eyes.

*   *   *

"Cheer up, dear, it'll soon be closing time."

Ashley jumped, as Mrs. O'Hara, one of Mr. White's most loyal customers, dumped a handful of dollars on the counter and waited patiently for her change.

"Oh, I'm sorry." Ashley smiled wanly. "I'm afraid I'm a bit of a zombie this afternoon."

She had been a zombie all day, ever since she'd woken from a disturbed sleep to remember, with crushing devastation—and a faint feeling of anger—that any faint hope she had ever entertained of making some kind of life with Gray was over. Permanently over.

But it was just as well that she had to work this afternoon. At least work forced her to keep half her mind on something other than the terrifying emptiness of the future. Or it had up until now.

"I'm sorry, Mrs. O'Hara," she repeated. "Thank you for coming in."

Mrs. O'Hara was the last customer. Twenty minutes later Ashley totaled her cash, shut the door behind her, and locked it.

"Hop in," said a voice.

"Oh!" She jumped, missing her footing, and ended up facedown in the snowbank beside the road.

As she scrambled to her feet with undignified haste, Ashley closed her eyes. Yesterday's scene with Gray must have curdled her mind. This wasn't possible. She was hallucinating. People couldn't open doors, expecting to step into snow, and end up stepping back into the past instead.

Or could they?

Slowly, not really wanting to shatter the illusion, she looked up.

This time Gray was still sitting in his car instead of helping to restore her equilibrium. But he was real.

"Hop in," he repeated.

"Why?" she asked. All her emotions were frozen and she was fighting an incredible sensation of déjà vu.

"Because I owe you an explanation."

That wasn't in the script. Last time they had played this scene he had been in no mood for explanations. In fact he had picked her up and dumped her into the car without ceremony.

"I don't think you owe me anything," she said wearily. An explanation wasn't what she wanted from Gray.

"I do. I've hurt you, and you have a right to know why."

"Does it matter why?"

"It matters to me."

This time she studied him more closely. There was still an ungiving harshness in the set of his mouth, and his jaw was tilted at that aggressive slant she knew so well. But today he couldn't, or wasn't trying, to disguise the deep emptiness in his eyes.

Without a word she stumbled through the dirty snow and sank onto the seat beside him.

"So I didn't have to kidnap you this time," he said. "I'm glad."

"Why are you glad? I thought you liked playing the buccaneer." It was easier to keep things on this flippant level. This way she didn't have to look at him. It was agony knowing he was here beside her, and that if she moved her hand just an inch or two she could touch his thigh. She mustn't do it, though. Extraordinary how in spite of everything, in spite of all the hurts and heartbreaks, just being near Gray could reduce her to this mindless heap of melting desire.

"I don't especially like 'playing the buccaneer,' as you put it," he replied, with a certain acidity. "But in your case I've found it effective."

"Not that effective," she replied tartly.

"True. But then I've never been a genuine buccaneer. Genuine buccaneers don't waste time asking for what they want. They take it."

"Is that what you're doing now?" asked Ashley, surprised to find she didn't really mind if it was. "Have I fallen into another trap?"

"Would that you had," he replied grimly. "Unfortunately I'd make a lousy pirate. I'm not much good at taking what isn't offered."

Ashley toyed vaguely with the idea of offering it, then discarded the notion almost at once. Gray might be ready to give her an explanation for his behavior, but he had said nothing about giving her his love. She bit her lip so hard that she almost drew blood, and stared glumly out of the window. But it didn't occur to her to wonder where they were going until she saw that they were pulling up outside his house.

"Is your father home?" she asked doubtfully, as he led her inside.

"No."

"Oh."

"He's playing bridge. And Mrs. Green's out too, if that was your next question."

"Oh," said Ashley again, because it was all she could manage before Daisy had her flattened against the wall.

Gray, his eyes curiously shuttered, perched himself on a corner of the kitchen table and watched the two of them greet each other with uninhibited affection.

"Lucky Daisy," he remarked, as the dog's nose rubbed joyfully against Ashley's cheek.

Gently Ashley pushed her friend down. "Good girl," she murmured. And then, briskly, to Gray, "I don't know why you brought me here, but let's get it over with quickly."

"Good Lord, what do you imagine I'm going to do to you? You make me sound like bad medicine—or worse."

Or better, thought Ashley unguardedly, watching the play of muscles as he hitched his hips more permanently on the edge of the table. She couldn't stand this much longer.

"Not medicine," she said hastily. "But I don't see what you hope to accomplish, so please get it off your chest so I can go home."

"You don't have to go home. Your mother isn't expecting you."

"Ah," Ashley nodded, as understanding dawned, "*that's* how you knew I was working! The Rosa Kalani family information network."

"Isn't that what mothers are for?"

"Not exactly," she replied dryly. But she remembered he hadn't had a mother, and said no more.

Gray moved away from the table then, and when he took her arm and glanced down at her for a moment she thought he was going to kiss her. She tensed, wanting him to, yet determined not to let him hurt her again. But the moment passed, and nothing happened.

"Come and sit down," he said, leading her into the living room. When she hesitated beside the sofa, he put a hand on her chest and pushed her into it, gently but very firmly. Then he sat down across from her in the tweed chair and stretched his legs, drawing her eyes to the snug fit of gray denim around his thighs.

"Well," she said, ignoring the annoying tightening in her breast, as well as a desperate longing to touch him, "why am I here?"

He smiled then, a slow, bitter smile. "For all the wrong reasons," he answered. "But as far as I'm concerned, you're here because yesterday I—didn't treat you with the consideration you deserved."

"Not unusual," Ashley couldn't help remarking.

He didn't even tell her to shut up. "No, not unusual, as you've frequently taken the trouble to point out." He put both hands behind his head and leaned back. "I apologize for that, Ashley. I don't know why you came to the office, but I had no business to treat you with less courtesy than I'd show to—oh, say the Dalton twins."

Ashley smiled bleakly. "It doesn't matter. And I came because your father said—said you wanted to see me, and that you were too stubborn to make the move yourself." There, it was out in the open.

"*Did* he now? The wily old buzzard. So that's why I kept imagining I could smell the scent of you on Daisy's fur." He lowered his arms and stood up suddenly, turning his back on her with an unconsciously feral movement. "That scent nearly drove me crazy, Ashley. And then, when you came into the office yesterday, I thought I really would go mad."

"I knew you weren't pleased."

"I wasn't. Just the same, I wanted to take you in my arms, to kiss that lost, unhappy look from your eyes. And because I couldn't do that——"

"You went into your Count Dracula act—according to your receptionist, that is."

"Did she say that? I suppose I haven't been giving poor Ann an easy time."

Ashley wondered if he ever gave anyone an easy time. "Why didn't you—kiss me?" she asked.

"For the same reason I said goodbye to you with no explanations—I thought it would make it easier for you to forget me. Ashley, I wanted you to hate me, so that you'd be able to carry on with your life with no regrets—no baggage from an old love to hold you back. I wanted—*want* you to be happy. I always will." She saw his fists whiten against his thighs.

"And you think I can be happy—hating you?" She couldn't believe what she was hearing.

"Why not? Plenty of people are." For a moment, as his fists clenched even tighter, she thought he was going to smash something. But he only lifted his head and strode stiffly across to the mantel. "You're in love with me, aren't you?" he said roughly, still with his back to her. When she drew a sharp breath and didn't reply, he went on in the same harsh voice, "I suspected it on Christmas Eve. That's why I sent you packing. Yesterday, when I saw your face, I was sure."

Ashley stared at his rigid back and wondered whether she should throw something at it, or throw her arms around his waist. In the end she did neither. "Yes," she admitted, twisting her fingers into a tight knot, "I do love you. I don't know how it happened. I didn't want it to, but it did." There was no point in dissembling any more.

"I'm sorry." Gray swung around and leaned back against the mantel. The fireplace behind him was as black and empty as his eyes.

"Why are you sorry?"

"Because no woman can love me and be happy. It's not in the cards." He was trying to make the words sound curt, factual. But Ashley knew him too well, and guessed they were wrenched from some personal hell that he had long ago come to terms with, but had no intention of sharing with her.

"I could be happy," she said quietly.

"No, you couldn't." His tone was hard. "But yesterday, after you left, I came to see that you were the sort of woman who stood a better chance of happiness—without me—if you understood *why* you can't love me. I suppose I've always known that really, but I kept fooling myself. I've grown too used to keeping my own counsel, to relationships that weren't meant to last..."

"So you didn't—send me packing, as you so graciously put it—just because I wouldn't sleep with you?" she said slowly.

"No, but I wanted you to think it."

"I did," she said simply. "But it didn't stop me loving you."

"Dear God." He closed his eyes. "Ashley..."

"It's all right, I do believe you meant it for the best. Now. So tell me the truth, Gray. Nothing about you can be so very terrible, can it?"

A muscle pulled tight in the hollow of his cheekbone, and he bowed his head. When he looked up again, he hooked his thumbs into his belt and said in a voice devoid of inflection, "I've a story to tell you, Ashley."

She nodded, shifting back on the sofa for more support. "Yes, tell me. Then perhaps you'll realize——"

"No, perhaps you'll realize."

He was glaring at her, so she bit her lip and waited for him to go on.

He began slowly, as if the words were being dragged out of him.

"You've met my father..."

"You know I have."

His eyes flashed with something that wasn't quite irritation. "Yes, all right. But you see there was a reason why I didn't want you to talk to him. I was afraid he'd bring up a subject I didn't want discussed——"

"He wouldn't have."

"Perhaps not. But you never know with him." He took a deep breath, and then continued almost as though he'd memorized a speech, "The point is, my father barely remembers *his* father. Both my grandparents died when he was very young, and the only thing he recollects clearly about his early years is being ill for quite a long time. Later he was adopted by a couple here in Thunder Bay. As my grandparents were immigrants from Ireland, he's never known anything about his family background, except that his adoptive parents were told there was a possibility his childhood illness had been an early symptom of a rare and debilitating disease—which as far as I can gather no one outside the medical profession has ever yet been able to pronounce." He smiled bleakly, and passed a hand over his face.

"What disease?" asked Ashley, holding her breath. She sensed that everything that had puzzled and confused her about Gray hung on his answer.

He told her.

And she couldn't pronounce it.

Neither could he, and his mouth twisted at the bitter irony.

"And—and it *was* a symptom?" she asked. "Is that why your father was in the hospital?"

"We still don't know." His voice grated like sandpaper on an open wound. "It's an odd disease, usually only strikes every second generation. Symptoms come and go, but it doesn't do a whole lot of damage until its victim reaches middle age, or later. Dad's been exceptionally healthy since he grew up, and his job at the mill kept him active, but there are no certainties with this plague, and, when he came down with sudden muscular stiffness and difficulty in walking just after I came home, naturally we thought . . ." He shrugged. "It's not hard to figure out what we thought."

"No," she agreed wryly. "And I suppose that happened the evening before I came into Boyko's and found you locked in mortal combat with the coffeemaker."

He winced. "No. He went into the hospital the day I met you, which, I have to admit, didn't improve my disposition. The coffeemaker incident came after we'd had some rather unfavorable results from his tests—since contradicted."

Things were beginning to fall into place, thought Ashley. "So you're still not sure——" she began.

"No, we're not sure. He's made a splendid recovery and the tests were inconclusive. But that proves nothing, either way."

She heard the bleakness in his voice and saw the lines deepen around his eyes even as he spoke, and she wanted desperately to jump up and fling her arms around him, to hold him and give him comfort. But she knew that if she did he would push her away. He regarded his family problems as his burden, not hers. He was used to them.

He was also used, she understood at last, to the long-term implications of what he had told her. That was why he had never made time for serious entanglements—why, when he realized her dream of roses had become a different dream, he had cast her off. Not because he wanted to.

He had done it for her.

A lump swelled in her chest, and threatened to burst. "I'm so sorry, Gray," she said quietly, knowing better than to offer useless platitudes.

"No reason why you should be. He's not your father."

Ashley sighed. "No, but I'm fond of him. And I'm not a fool, Gray. I can see that it must be hell for you—to live with the knowledge that, although it probably won't strike *you*, if it does exist in your family it could affect any children you may have."

He spun around with such violence that she jumped to her feet, while Daisy scuttled into a corner.

"Ashley," he said, maintaining his control with what was obviously an effort, "Ashley, don't you realize there won't *be* any children? That's what I'm trying to tell you. I can't produce kids for my own egotistical satisfaction and then condemn them to live with that plague hanging over their heads. Even *I'm* not that selfish—whatever you may think."

Ashley's legs went weak, and for a moment she was afraid she was going to fall. Not because of his stinging impatience with her, but because she understood what it must have cost him over the years to come to terms with his "plague." She knew he loved children. He was a born father. But of course fatherhood was an experience he could never have. And, being Gray, he would inevitably decide that meant he couldn't marry—or even commit himself—because that would be inflicting the burden he had always borne alone on the one he loved.

"Gray," she said, controlling the trembling in her limbs with great difficulty, "Gray, is that why you said I couldn't love you? Why you said no woman could love you?"

"Yes," he replied, with a quiet acceptance that made her want to cry. "If I can't condemn my children to that uncertainty, what right have I to condemn the woman I love to a lifetime of childlessness?" He turned away from her, propped an elbow on the mantel, and rested his forehead on his hand.

Ashley, suppressing an unworthy impulse to remark that a lifetime without children couldn't be all bad, took a step toward him and then stopped. "So you sent me away," she said tonelessly. "Just as you sent all the others. You didn't even give us a chance."

He lifted his head then and smiled wearily. "I was certain that's what you'd say if you knew. That's why I wanted you to hate me."

When she only stared at him, too numbed to reply, he added flatly, "There weren't any others."

"Gray, please——"

"I mean there weren't any others I needed to send away. They went of their own accord."

"Because you wouldn't let them get close to you," said Ashley with a shattering certainty.

"I suppose so. But it didn't seem to matter much—until a few months ago."

"What happened to make it matter?" she asked, so dazed by Gray's revelations that she couldn't think clearly any more.

"Don't you know?"

She shook her head.

"You know, I honestly believe you don't."

As if he were being forced against his will, Gray moved toward her. "Ashley. My sweet Ashley," he said hoarsely. "Hasn't it been as obvious as the broken nose on my face that everything changed that day I walked into

Boyko's? I saw your charming bottom decorating the top of a ladder, and nothing has been the same since."

Ashley choked back a laugh that was almost a sob. "Does that mean——?"

"It means I love you, Ashley Kalani. I can't marry you, I can't let you waste your life on me, but more than anything in the world I want you to be happy. I was a blind idiot to believe you when you said that all you wanted was a home of your own and a good job. I thought all I had to do was persuade you into my bed, and both our problems would be solved. By the time I realized, in a flash of belated brilliance on Christmas Eve, that a nice bit of bed could never be enough for either of us, it was too late. You'd fallen in love with me, as I had with you. I suppose that's why I was such a—what was it you called me?"

"Rat? Bastard? Jekyll and Hyde?" said Ashley helpfully.

"Okay, okay," his smile was rueful, "I didn't ask for a catalog. But you see I had to fight what I was feeling, every inch of the way. And, even so, in the end it was no good—the only thing I could do for you was hurt you. Or so I believed—until I saw your sweet face in my office yesterday."

"Idiot!"

Gray blinked. "What did you say?"

"I said idiot."

"That's what I thought." He was standing only a few inches from her, and she read disbelief and indignation in his eyes, as well as bewilderment. He had just spoken the words that more than any others she had longed to hear, but he looked so out of his depth, so uncharacteristically confused, that to her own confusion, Ashley had trouble stifling a chuckle.

"You're an idiot to think I can't love you just because you can't have children," she explained, taking pity on him. "Kids are wonderful—or so my mother keeps telling me—but at the moment I'm still in college. And I haven't totally given up my dream of enjoying peace and privacy for a few years. If—if—well, if in the future I were— um..." She took a long breath, not wanting to bring up the fatal word marriage. "If I were *committed* to someone, and I decided I was ready to have children, which I'm sure will happen one day——"

"That's exactly what I said," Gray snapped. "I know you like kids. Look at the way you are with your brothers and sisters, even when you're threatening to murder them. Why do you think I didn't want you to know about my—deficiencies? It wasn't male pride, my dear—I've long outgrown that. It was the knowledge that, sweet and wonderful as you are, you would have willingly given up your chance of a normal family life to make me happy. I couldn't allow that." He scowled so ferociously that Ashley lifted a hand to smooth his brow.

"Let me finish," she insisted. "When and if the day comes that I want children, what's wrong with adopting? You're wonderful with other people's children, Gray..."

"It's not always that easy." He was still scowling, but the gap between their bodies was closing imperceptibly.

"Perhaps not. But Gray, I love you. You said you loved me. Any obstacle can be overcome if we care enough, if we're willing to surmount it together. Whatever happens, we'll have—I mean we *would* have each other."

She raised her eyes, afraid of what she would see in his, afraid that his lifetime rejection of intimacy had grown too deep. And when she met the velvet intensity of his gaze she was still afraid.

But his hands gripped her shoulders and very slowly he pulled her against his chest. Then, for a few seconds, she believed she would never be afraid again.

"Ashley," he murmured, before his lips closed over hers with such tender passion that the earth really did seem to move beneath her feet. "Ashley, how could I have been such a fool?"

"Well, you've never found *that* difficult," she commented, as she moved her mouth lovingly against his cheek.

"Witch!" He slid his hands lingeringly over her bottom, rocking his hips against hers as he began to bite gently at her neck.

After that neither of them said anything until Daisy, tired of being neglected and taking a very dim view of the antics of two people she thought should be replenishing her food dish, projected herself across the carpet with ears flying, and knocked them both flat onto the floor.

"Well," said Gray, as he pulled them to a sitting position and put his arm around her waist, "I suppose we could be in a worse situation."

"What do you mean?"

"Just that I always thought proposals were made with the man down on one knee, and the woman sitting demurely in a chair with her hands folded. At the moment I'm on my backside, and you're sitting on what's left of my lunch. Also that ridiculous dog appears to think I'm proposing to her."

Daisy wriggled her long body ecstatically and rested her head on Gray's shoulder.

"And are you?" asked Ashley, giving up all thought of ever catching her breath again.

"Am I what?"

"Proposing to Daisy."

"No, I'm proposing to you. If you really meant what you said about our always having each other, will you make that official? Will you marry me, Ashley, and say goodbye to your dream of peace and privacy in a cottage covered with roses?" His voice was soft, seductive and irresistible, but his eyes betrayed the uncertainty in his heart.

"It wouldn't be a dream if you weren't in it," said Ashley, lifting her hand tenderly to his cheek. "It would be a nightmare."

She saw the muscles move in his throat. "Does that mean yes?"

"Oh, Gray, dear Gray, how could you possibly doubt it?"

Ashley watched the shadows drop slowly from his face, and suddenly he seemed much younger. "Habit," he said, smiling crookedly. "I've grown accustomed to doubts over the years. But I'll never be able to doubt you, my Ashley."

She smiled back dreamily, gave a long sigh of happiness, and linked her arms about his neck.

Daisy grunted, gave a long sigh of disgust, and sat on his feet.

"I think we'd better adjourn to the sofa," said Gray a short while later. "Or with this combined assault on my circulation I may never survive to walk you down the aisle!"

They adjourned, and Daisy, giving her best impression of an offended carpet, stalked reproachfully back to her corner.

"Are you really sure?" asked Gray, pulling Ashley onto his knee.

"Sure of what?"

"Sure that you won't mind. About children."

"Oh, Gray, of course I'm sure! Besides..." She hesitated, not sure how he might react. "Besides, your father had you, didn't he? And that wasn't a total disaster."

He frowned. "Ashley, if that's what you're hoping——"

"It isn't. I just wondered why——"

"I was an accident," he interrupted gruffly. "I appeared late in life when I wasn't supposed to be possible."

"Well, you're not very possible, are you?" she said mildly, smoothing a wave of dark hair off his forehead.

Gray choked, and the scowl faded. "I suppose not," he admitted ruefully. "And as a matter of fact Dad was delighted when I showed up, accident or no accident, so I never felt unwanted. But he was determined that, since I couldn't expect immortality the usual way, I'd have to look for it in a different direction."

"Hockey?"

"Mmm."

"The Hockey Hall of Fame. And did you like it, or were you always under pressure?"

"If I was, I didn't realize it. I enjoyed the game. The pressure grew from inside myself when I was older, and I really didn't bother to analyze it much. I suppose the life-style suited me. I'd always known marriage and permanency weren't in the cards for me, and I didn't mind. It was a good excuse to play the field. Until I walked into Boyko's, and bought it because I met you."

"Did you? Was *that* why?"

"Well, don't let your head get too swollen. I was considering it anyway, because I had to stick around Thunder Bay with Dad. But your delicious bottom clinched the deal." He pulled her against him and gave the bottom in question a playful slap.

"Oh, Gray," whispered Ashley, quite overcome, "so *that's* why you kept coming into the shop when you didn't need to!"

"Why else?" He curled his fingers in her hair and pulled her face roughly against his.

When they finally came up for air some time later, he rested his hand on her thigh and said slowly, "There is one thing, Ashley. One ray of hope."

"What's that?"

"You see, this disease—it's one they haven't known much about until recently. But a few months ago they isolated the gene, which takes them that much closer to a cure. So ten years from now—who knows? Miracles do happen." His eyes met hers, suddenly challenging. "But there's no point counting on it."

"Gray, I'm *not* counting on it," said Ashley, exasperated. "If it happens, that's wonderful, and not just for you and me. But I've told you, all I want now is *you*, and later, although I know it may not be easy, we'll overcome our problems together."

His face cleared, and Ashley heaved a sigh of relief. It looked as though at last he was beginning to accept that she was as capable as he was of looking the future squarely in the eye and facing up to it—as he had always been forced to do. She knew he would continue to have his doubts, but with time she was sure they would lessen, and in the end he would learn to believe that for her, whatever happened, he, Gray McGraw, would be enough.

"Can I be a bridesmaid?" shouted Gina.

Rocky snickered. "Yeah, and maybe Nick and Carlo can be ring bearers—in cute velvet suits."

"Yuck," muttered Carlo.

"No way," scoffed Nick. "It's bad enough having Ash and Gray going all slobbery over each other. And I suppose nobody's going to talk anything but wedding talk for weeks and weeks."

Gray grinned. "Don't worry, Nick, I don't think I could stand that either. So Ashley and I are going to be married next week, very quietly. Then she's coming to live with me and Dad until we find a place of our own."

"Why can't you live here?" asked Nick, visions of endless sports talk apparently dancing in his head.

"Because your mother has quite enough to do looking after you lot," said Gray firmly, catching sight of Rosa's startled face. "And Ashley has her final exams coming up soon. She needs quiet."

"We'd be quiet," said Nick, never one to give up without a fight.

Ashley made a noise that was part groan and part snort, and Gray glanced at her quizzically. On the whole, he thought, she was bearing up very well under the combined onslaughts of her sisters, who wanted to hear every last detail of his proposal, her parents, who regarded the hasty wedding with a certain skepticism, and her brothers, who looked on the whole thing with deep suspicion—except for Rocky, who looked on it as an opportunity to tease anyone who would rise to his bait.

They had told Bruce McGraw their good news when he arrived home from bridge the previous night. He had been positively puffed with triumph, convinced that he had engineered the happy turn of events single-handed—as perhaps he had. But they had waited until late the following afternoon to tell Ashley's family, because Ashley said she needed time to prepare herself for the inevitable clamor. Not to mention the probable objections of her parents, who would want them to wait until they could have a big, noisy wedding.

As it turned out, Ashley was mistaken about that. Toivo had no objection to saving money, and Rosa harbored a strong notion that the marriage had been consummated prematurely and ought to be made legal at once.

In that, Rosa was wrong. Gray and Ashley had sat up very late after his father came home and, almost shyly, Ashley had belatedly offered him the Christmas gift that once he had almost demanded.

He had refused.

"No, sweet Ashley," he replied softly. "After I've waited all my life for you, it won't hurt me to wait one week longer." He smiled. "It may kill me, but it won't hurt me."

There was such a wealth of love in his eyes that Ashley had to bury her face in his shoulder to hide the tears he might not understand.

"Come on, all of you," said Rosa, watching the two of them now with a small smile. "Out! Ashley and Gray want to be alone."

To Ashley's amazement, in three seconds flat the living room was deserted. "Wow!" she exclaimed, as Sophia's voice receded down the hall complaining loudly that it wasn't fair that Maria should be the only one to get a room to herself. "You must be a miracle worker, Gray. Mom didn't even have to yell!"

"Bribery," he said smugly. "I slipped them all tickets to the Flyers game while you were out in the kitchen. They figure they owe me one."

Ashley laughed. "I might have known! You ought to watch it, though. If you don't come across with the goods so easily another time, Nick's not above blackmail."

"And I'm not above administering a swift kick in the right place, so I wouldn't worry about it."

"I wasn't," replied Ashley dryly, thinking that she was incapable of worrying about anything much while he was smiling down at her with that slow, seductive smile that curled her toes.

"Good." He sank into the nearest chair, pulling her with him. "Ashley...?"

"Mmm?" She rubbed her thumb gently over his lower lip. He caught it, and held both her hands against his chest.

"Ashley, I've been thinking. You know what I'd like to do?"

"Make love to me?" she suggested.

"That too," he agreed with a grin, dropping his hand to give her a possessive pat on the thigh. "But *after* that—well, at the same time as that—I'd like to set up a rehabilitation clinic for injured kids..."

"You mean injured in sporting accidents?" she asked, eyes widening.

"Not necessarily. Just a clinic for children. I have the capital, I could staff it with qualified people, and, although I suppose it sounds arrogant, with my name I wouldn't have any trouble raising funds.''

"No," said Ashley, "you wouldn't. It doesn't sound arrogant, just practical." She hesitated. "Would you actually want to run it yourself?"

"Yes, I think I would. Once I've got Boyko's straightened around, it will pretty much run itself. I've been mulling this one over for a long time, but up until yesterday I hadn't any hope that my brainchild might include you. Want a job, Ashley Kalani? As the clinic's administrator? You'd be perfect, especially as I'd like to concentrate quite a lot of my time on the kids. I think I can help them, because I know what it's like to be confined to bed day after day, wondering if you'll ever get back on your feet." His eyes clouded briefly. "I can't stand to see kids in that situation."

Ashley knew he was remembering all the torment he had lived through in the past—weeks and months that she couldn't even imagine.

"Oh, Gray!" She jumped to her feet, too overwhelmed to keep still. "Oh, Gray, it's a wonderful idea! It's exactly the sort of job I hoped for, and now I won't even have to look for work."

"No," he agreed, rising purposefully from the chair and coming to take her back in his arms, "you won't. And if anyone tries to hire you away from me, I'll break his neck."

"I don't *think*," said Ashley pensively, "that that would be a very good idea."

"I don't see why not."

"Because respectable directors of rehabilitation clinics aren't supposed to create customers for other clinics. It just isn't done."

"Isn't it? Then let's hope no one ever attempts to steal you."

"They couldn't," said Ashley simply. "I wouldn't let them."

Gray's arms tightened around her. "Neither would I," he murmured into her ear. "And don't you forget it."

As she sank blissfully against him, the door behind them burst open, and Nick's disgusted voice exclaimed, "Oh, boy, they're at it again! And you know what, Carlo? That weird glass bowl of Mom's you nearly broke has done something funny. It's made a rainbow on the floor right by their feet."

With a muffled groan, Gray held Ashley away from him. But when they looked down they saw that it was true.

Just where they stood, the afternoon sun shining through the cut-glass bowl had cast a delicate rainbow at their feet.

"Do you believe in omens?" asked Gray, his eyes smiling tenderly into hers.

"Of course." Ashley held out her arms.

The two of them, ignoring their audience, continued their interrupted embrace, and Nick turned to his brother and said hopelessly, "It's no good, Carlo. I don't think Gray's going to talk about sports at all this afternoon."

He was right.

Gray wasn't.

Let

HARLEQUIN ROMANCE®
take you

BACK TO THE

Come to the Monarch Ranch and the Crazy Ace,
near Addison, Wyoming

Meet Jim Trent, Addison County's favorite son—rodeo
superstar turned rancher. He's a classic man of the West.
You'll *also meet* Suzannah Glenn, daughter of Addison's
richest rancher—and a woman who knows what she wants.
But watch out! Suzannah's got a romantic streak, especially
when it comes to wild horses. And wilder cowboys!

Read WILD HORSES by Ruth Jean Dale,
bestselling author of The Taggarts of Texas series, including
FIREWORKS! and SHOWDOWN!

Available in May 1994
wherever Harlequin books are sold.

RANCH12

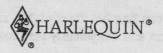

Where do you find hot Texas nights, smooth Texas charm and dangerously sexy cowboys?

Crystal Creek reverberates with the exciting rhythm of Texas.
Each story features the rugged individuals who live and love in the
Lone Star State.

"...Crystal Creek wonderfully evokes the hot days and steamy nights of
a small Texas community...impossible to put down until the last page
is turned."
—*Romantic Times*

"...a series that should hook any romance reader. Outstanding."
—*Rendezvous*

Praise for Bethany Campbell's *The Thunder Rolls*

"Bethany Campbell takes the reader into the minds of her characters so
surely...one of the best Crystal Creek books so far. It will be hard to
top...."

Don't miss the next book in this exciting series. Look for
RHINESTONE COWBOY by BETHANY CAMPBELL

Available in May wherever Harlequin books are sold.